I0614830

The Duke's Denial

by

Carolina Prescott

Dukes in Danger:
A Haversham House Romance

The Duke's Denial

Cover Art by *The Wild Rose Press, Inc.*

The Wild Rose Press, Inc.
PO Box 708
Adams Basin, NY 14410-0708
Visit us at www.thewildrosepress.com

Publishing History
First Edition, 2025
Trade Paperback ISBN 978-1-5092-6072-0
Digital ISBN 978-1-5092-6073-7

Dukes in Danger:A Haversham House Romance
Published in the United States of America

Dedication

For REK,
who always has the best answers
and knows how to make me smile.

Acknowledgments

My thanks as always to Nan, my wonderful editor and the most patient woman in the world.

~*~

Books by Carolina Prescott
in the Dukes in Danger series of
Haversham House Romances
The Duke's Decision, Book 1
The Duke's Dilemma, Book 2
The Duke's Defense, Book 3
The Duke's Denial, Book 4
published by The Wild Rose Press, Inc.

~*~

Praise for Carolina Prescott
The Duke's Decision was a winner in the Historical Romance category in the 2019 Fiction From the Heartland contest of the Mid America Romance Authors in Kansas City.

Chapter 1

December 1815

"*Must* you stand so close?"

"I was here first, my lady. If you don't want to be close to me, then I suggest *you* move."

"I am standing *precisely* where I am supposed to be." Lady Genevieve Richards, daughter of the late Earl of Tangier, whispered loudly while still smiling at the assembled crowd. "May I remind you, *I* am the maid of honor. I assist the bride with her bouquet and veil and *you* are in the way, your grace."

Eve—as she was known to anyone who knew her at all—met the dark gray eyes of Hill Barbour, the Duke of Camberton and then quickly looked away. Hill, for once, was impeccably dressed, and, as one might expect, looked amazing in the formal morning attire that well-bred gentlemen wore for such important events. For some reason his undeniable good looks irritated Eve further.

"May I remind you, madam," said Hill in his best stage whisper, "that *I* am the best man? I have the rings, I make sure the groom arrives on time, and I bear witness to the events." Disregarding the narrowing eyes of the lady at his side, the duke continued, "As best man, I have the responsibility—nay, the *duty*—to ensure that the bride finds her way to her future husband and, I might add, my best friend, unimpeded."

"It's a fairly straight path down the aisle," muttered Eve just loud enough for Hill to hear. "I feel certain she'll be able to navigate the journey on her own." She jabbed a sharp elbow into Camberton's side in yet another effort to move him back and away from her. "And *must* you always tower over people so?"

"Ow!" said Hill, catching the offending appendage before it could retreat from whence it came. "That hurt! I cannot help that your lack of height is made more evident by my own stature."

"Let go of me!" hissed Eve, pulling away.

Just two steps away, the groom, unwilling to take his eyes off his beautiful bride—who at that very moment was starting down the center aisle of London's second-most important church on her father's arm—turned his head a fraction of a degree toward his best man and his fiancée's maid of honor. "If the two of you don't shut it right now, I swear on everything that's holy I will put you in Haversham's dungeon for a month—together!"

Eve continued to glare up at Hill but held her tongue. Avery was right. This was not the time to air her grievances or take out her anger and frustration. This was Linney and Avery's wedding day, and it was her job—and Hill's job, she admitted grudgingly to herself—to ensure that everything proceeded perfectly for the wedding of Miss Linea Braddock to the new Duke of Easton.

There would be plenty of time for confrontations after the ceremony.

It was only four short months ago that Eve had met the Duke of Camberton. He was as handsome then as he was today, although then his attire had been a little less formal. Also, he was writhing on the ground in the barnyard of the Dog and Pony Inn, covered in what one hoped was merely mud. His was an understandably instinctive response to a well-placed knee to the ducal…ah, nether regions—something which Eve was certain she had apologized for on more than one occasion.

Almost certain.

Eve could be forgiven for not remembering for, at the time, she was yelling at the top of her voice and calling his grace every foul name she could think of—which turned out to be quite a few, considering her rather sheltered upbringing. By the time Avery and Linney arrived to rescue Hill and belatedly make the Duke of Camberton known to her, Eve had already ascertained that, not only was the duke quite tall and quite muscular—a refreshing change from most of the other male members of the aristocracy to whom she had been introduced by her mother over this past year—but he was also quite attractive and would undoubtedly be even more so when standing upright and not covered in mud.

The other thing she learned about Camberton that day was that he knew how to hold a grudge.

After the misunderstanding had been corrected and proper introductions had been made, Eve was more than happy to let bygones be bygones and quite willing to forgive Hill's mistaking her for a servant boy. But Camberton was not nearly as gracious. He seemed to think that simply because Eve was dressed as a stable boy and had just emerged from the barn of the aforementioned inn with straw on her clothes and her hair tucked up under a cap, he could dispense with common courtesies and treat her like some sort of hired help—which, to be fair, was exactly what she was at the time,

Hill finally did accept her apology, but he also made a point of keeping his distance from Eve. Who knows how long he would have avoided her had they not, just the very next day, found themselves in danger of being discovered by none other than the notorious Monsieur Jones, Napoleon's cunning and extremely dangerous spymaster—a ruthless man who had eluded British authorities for years.

Eve couldn't remember exactly when it was that she first fell in love with Hill—whether it was when she saw him doubled over on the ground in front of her, or if it happened that next day when she found herself being held tightly in his arms as they hid from Jones.

They spent the next several weeks together—supposedly playing chaperone for their betrothed friends at Terra Bella, the Duke of Easton's country home. In reality, however, *they* were the ones in need of a chaperone as they fell hopelessly and completely in love—at least that's what Eve remembered.

Toward the end of that blissful summer, Camberton received an urgent message from the Duke of Whitley to return to London. Before he left, Hill asked if he might write to her.

"That would be lovely," said Eve after a particularly long and meltingly passionate kiss. "But won't you be busy? When will you have time to write to me?"

Hill answered with another kiss. "Every day," he whispered into her ear.

"That was exactly the right answer," sighed Eve, already anticipating an autumn full of long love letters and ardent declarations and, eventually, a proposal of marriage. She knew it would be hard to be separated from Hill, but she also knew they would be together again at the end of the year for Avery and Linney's New Year's Eve wedding. Eve smiled as she waved goodbye, determined to make the parting easier for Hill by holding back her tears until he was out of sight.

But no love letters from Hill ever arrived. In fact, there was no word of any kind—no explanation, no regrets, no nothing. Nothing until she saw him last evening at Haversham House.

Eve couldn't remember exactly when she fell in love with Hill, but she remembered exactly the day she commanded herself to fall *out* of love with him. That would be yesterday—more specifically, last night at dinner when he barely acknowledged her presence as he flirted unceasingly with both Miss Banbury and Lady Amelia and—

The bride cleared her throat and Eve started guiltily. She was supposed to be holding Linney's bouquet while her friend said her vows. Smiling an apology, Eve took the bouquet of red roses and lacy white baby's breath. Ignoring Hill's smirk, she resolved anew to focus all her attention on making this day perfect for her two friends.

****

Seeing Eve come down the aisle—hell, seeing her at all—made him ache in a way he'd not felt since summer. He had the same physical reaction he always had in seeing her, but he also had the heartache of knowing how much he'd hurt her. She was so beautiful and so proud and—as parts of his body were inconveniently reminding him—a rather excellent student in foreplay. Where *had* she developed such skills? It was a question he would very much enjoy finding the answer to, but first things first. Right now, he needed to focus on making it through his best friend's wedding without embarrassing himself and without compromising his undercover persona.

And then he had to find out the identity of the infamous Monsieur Jones.

Chapter 2

Eve resolutely turned her eyes to the groom. Avery's face was filled with wonder as he feasted his eyes on his true love in her wedding finery. Linney was absolutely gorgeous in her candlelight satin gown with its fashionable empire waist. The gown's bodice was heavily embroidered with crystal beads sparkling in an intricate design that incorporated a stylized yew tree from the Easton family crest. The pattern, designed by Linney's mother, was repeated along the border of the bride's long train. Linney's cornsilk blonde hair was piled high, held in place with diamond encrusted combs—a wedding gift from Avery. A few errant tendrils kissed her neck under her veil of the finest Brussels lace. Linney's bridal clothes were truly breathtaking, but it was her smile, full of love for her groom, that was the most beautiful part of her ensemble.

From confidences that she'd shared with Linney, Eve knew that Avery had already seen a great deal more of his bride than was proper, but the look on his face was something Eve would remember forever. Awe, pride, and disbelief, along with something akin to possessiveness and unbridled lust, combined to create a look of love that shone like the sun.

"*That*," thought Eve to herself, "that is what *I* want. I want a man who looks at me like *that*." In her mind's eye, she pictured herself in a lacy, white gown standing beside a gentle, refined man with tousled, golden locks and gazing directly into pale blue eyes that looked deep into her soul. Her dream groom was *not* overly tall or dark or brooding, with eyes that flashed black when he was angry or in pain.

Or kissing her.

No, the man she wanted to marry wrote odes to her lips and sonnets to her eyes—he didn't block her path or elbow her to the side so he could have a better view. He was someone who knew and understood her every thought, her desires, and all of her dreams. A partner and a soulmate, yes, but also a considerate husband—who respected her intelligence and encouraged her passion for mapping the world. And in return, Eve would treasure her beloved's every word, basking in his wisdom and goodness. Together they would live in perfect harmony with never an angry word or raised voice as they—

"Hill! Stop it!" she hissed.

Trying to improve his position, Avery's best man had inadvertently pushed against Eve's shoulder, interrupting her from her reverie and throwing her off balance. She grabbed for his arm as she lurched sideways—stepping on his foot by accident, but grinding her heel into that same foot very much on purpose.

Hill's dark eyes flashed as he stifled an outcry and glared at Eve. He stepped forward to put the two plain gold bands into the open hand of the archbishop and then retreated back to his position, sending one more scowl in Eve's direction.

Ignoring Camberton, but acutely aware of Avery's disapproving glare, Eve stood like a statue, a hastily acquired angelic smile beaming as the cleric blessed the rings and offered the first one to Avery to give to his bride.

"With this ring, I thee wed…"

Linney already wore the beautiful Easton family betrothal ring that Avery had given her this past summer—the summer when Linney and Eve had first crossed paths and become fast friends. Now, as she listened to Avery repeat the timeless words to his bride, her eyes misted. What would it feel like, she wondered, to be so in love with someone—someone who was so in love with you?

A handkerchief appeared from thin air. Fine white linen with the Camberton crest embroidered in the corner. Eve snatched it and dabbed at her eyes as Linney put the other gold band on Avery's finger and recited her promise to him.

Eve felt rather than heard Hill clear his throat. She glanced up and caught him looking down at her with a tenderness that pierced her heart. Their eyes met, and for a brief second it was as if they were back at Terra Bella and the last four months had never happened. Confused, she turned quickly back to the ceremony. But as Linney continued her vows, Eve couldn't help glancing up at Hill again.

"With my body I thee worship…"

This time Hill boldly met her eyes with a leer, waggling his eyebrows at the words of the service. Eve rolled her eyes and looked away. He was *such* a rogue. She must have mistaken his earlier expression. How could she ever have believed herself in love with him? The sooner she could get away from the Duke of Camberton, the better.

Chapter 3

The ceremony was over at last.

It was a special kind of torture to be standing so close to the woman you loved and not be able to talk to her or hold her in your arms. It was bad enough having to listen to the words of the marriage ceremony knowing that the words were not being said for him and his Eve. And perhaps never would be. All he could do was smell that honeysuckle scent she wore and remember.

It was amazing to Hill how his world view had changed since becoming a duke—or more correctly, since becoming a duke and meeting Eve. He had not been raised to take on the mantle of aristocracy that he now wore. His branch of the family tree had splintered generations ago when his great-grandfather married beneath his station and was shunned by the more noble limbs. After university, Hill went to London with Avery, his boyhood friend and the Duke of Easton's one and only heir. Later that same year, however, he and Avery had a falling out—over a woman, of course—and Hill bought a commission in His Majesty's Army. He was immediately deployed to the continent to fight Napoleon, where he earned a commendation and a command of his own. He was genuinely respected by both the officers and the enlisted men whom he commanded, and his strategic capabilities were noticed by those who mattered in the chain of command.

Soon after his second promotion, Hill was recruited by the Duke of Whitley to become part of his covert network of intelligence gatherers. In other words, Hill became a spy for the Crown. It was during that same time when he received word that he was the new Duke of Camberton and actually had been for almost a year—ever since a terrible boating accident claimed the life of a distant cousin in a family that regularly produced more females than males. Hill was alerted to his new role by a one-line message received on his last day as a battlefield commander from a London solicitor who specialized in letters patent. The ducal inheritance changed nothing at the time, and everything for his future.

Despite his outwardly gregarious personality, the Duke of Camberton was actually a loner. Perhaps it was a reaction to growing up as a twin and having never been alone in his life until he left for college. He soon found that he enjoyed solitude and relished his time alone, telling himself that he neither wanted nor needed anyone else in his life. Other than his sister, Henrianna, the only other person he'd ever really been close to was Avery.

All of that changed when he was formally introduced to Lady Genevieve Richards in the barnyard of the Dog and Pony Inn.

From the very first day they met, Hill knew that he wanted Eve in his life. Like his twin sister, Lady Eve was feisty and outspoken, but that's where the similarity ended. While Hen was tall like himself, Eve was a tiny thing. As he recalled, she fit perfectly under his chin, allowing him to kiss her hair and breathe in her delicately sweet scent.

Hill knew that he wanted to spend his life with Eve, but even he hadn't expected there to be so many detours and so many obstacles standing between them. He certainly had not anticipated that the secrecy surrounding his work for the Duke of Whitley would necessitate a total ban on any communications between Eve and himself.

Hill was at Terra Bella with Avery, Linney, and Eve when he received the late-summer order from the Duke of Whitley. Whit, as he and Avery had always called Avery's half-brother, was known throughout the *ton* as the Ice Duke because of his condescending and rather forbidding manner. Only a select few knew that the Duke of Whitley was, in fact, the King's spymaster and the man who oversaw a vast network of operatives and informants both inside and outside the country.

Up until Napoleon's second abdication and subsequent banishment to Saint Helena in June of 1815, the Duke of Whitley and his web of spies had been singularly focused in their efforts to bring down the self-anointed emperor as he rampaged across the continent. Napoleon's defeat at the hands of Great Britain and her allies at Waterloo marked the end of his reign and should also have seen the end of his spymaster. Credited as the mastermind behind many of Napoleon's victories, Monsieur Jones refused to accept Napoleon's defeat and, according to credible intelligence from Whit's sources, was now trying to recruit and organize like-minded individuals to bring Napoleon back to power yet again—even as Jones systematically eliminated anyone who dared express doubt about the Corsican's ability to reclaim his empire. Jones remained at large, primarily because no one knew his real identity. Rumors claimed that the man teetered on the edge of insanity—making him even more dangerous than before.

Earlier in the year, Jones had kidnapped Vivian, Lady Rowden, now the Duke of Whitley's duchess. Jones had planned to present the lady to Napoleon as England's brilliant codemaker and a kind of trophy. However, when the Duke of Whitley successfully orchestrated Vivian's rescue, it marked the beginning of the end for Napoleon. Rightly or wrongly, the emperor blamed his final defeat on his spymaster and the foiled kidnapping, and Jones had ultimately been shunned by his beloved leader. For such a loyal acolyte, there could be no greater disgrace, and Jones set out to exact his own revenge on those he believed responsible for Napoleon's downfall and his own fall from grace: the Ice Duke, his duchess, and his associates.

Time and time again, Jones had demonstrated his cold-blooded efficiency in silencing his own people once they had served his purpose. Whit confessed that, in all his years of service to the Crown, he had never seen such callous disregard for human life. If this was how Jones treated his *own* people, one could only imagine what he would do to his sworn enemies.

When Whit ordered Hill to London, it had been to start a new, highly secret mission to find out the truth about Monsieur Jones. Apart from rumors that Jones was a member of the British aristocracy, little else was known about the man. At least one credible source pointed to Lord Glenly, an English viscount, as holding the key to Jones' true identity. However, while Whit believed the viscount knew a great deal more about Jones than he let on, Glenly came from a long line of noblemen who had always been loyal supporters of the monarchy, so any attempt to accuse him of a traitorous connection to Jones had to be done quietly and with incontrovertible proof.

Which is why, in August, Whit sent a message to the Duke of Camberton that took him away from his summer activities and brought him to London.

Chapter 4

Hill and Eve had been on the verge of something very special. Before he left Terra Bella, Hill promised to write to Eve as soon and as often as possible. As he rode away, he mentally calculated how long it would be before he could ask for her hand in marriage and to whom he might address his intentions. Once Hill reached London, however, things changed.

The mission that Whit needed Hill for was highly confidential and required Camberton to take on the guise of a womanizing, ne'er-do-well duke, a role he had aspired to in a previous life. The top-secret challenge required Hill to sever all ties to his recent life, including his relationship with Eve. He was not allowed to explain or even send the briefest message to her, which meant he had not communicated with her since that day in late August when he said goodbye.

If the Duke of Camberton had any sense at all, he would have asked Avery to find someone else to serve as his best man on his wedding day so that he and Eve would not be thrown together in so many wedding-related activities. Ironically, it was Whit who gave permission for Hill to go through with his part in the wedding, rationalizing that serving as Avery's best man would enhance Camberton's cover story. Typically, Whit had no thought for how Hill's charade would affect Eve.

Or Hill himself.

If he closed his eyes, Hill could actually smell Eve's light honeysuckle scent and feel her melting in his arms as she returned his kisses and came apart under his purposeful caresses. The mere thought of being close to her made his body harden. It had been difficult enough to be away from her since August, but being so close to her now and not being able to give her any reason or explanation for his odd and most ungentlemanly behavior had tormented his heart. He dreaded seeing the look of betrayal in her eyes. Certainly she could not have been looking forward to seeing *him.*

The truth of the matter was that he'd been desperate to see her again—under any circumstances—but now he was confused. The spitfire who had just ground her sharp heel into the tenderest part of his foot didn't seem to be nursing any signs of unrequited love. For the first time, Hill wondered if he had misread her feelings for him during their late-summer interlude.

As he listened to Linney and Avery saying their vows, Hill's eyes met Eve's and for just an instant he couldn't hide his love for her. He saw the hurt in her eyes—a hurt he'd put there—and he longed to pull her into his arms and whisper the same promises that Avery was making to Linney.

Thank heavens she quickly looked away. The next time she glanced his way, Hill had managed to get his emotions back under control, and he flashed a lascivious grin—exactly what one would expect from his acquired persona.

****

At the front of the church, the bishop gestured to

Hill. The cleric was trying to shepherd everyone into the tiny room off to the side so they could sign the registry. Hill entered first and flattened himself against the wall at the far end of the room. Unfortunately, his actions left some space, and the bishop directed Eve to stand directly in front of him. As the rest of the wedding party gathered into the small room, someone stumbled, starting a chain reaction that had the effect of pushing Eve right into Hill's arms.

Bloody hell! Did she wash her hair with that honeysuckle soap?

He couldn't help holding her close for a moment. She fit perfectly in his arms, just as he remembered. For a few precious seconds she belonged to him again. He didn't say a word, but she must have felt how his body welcomed her in spite of his best efforts, and she must have heard his heart beating wildly.

And then the oddest thing happened—at least he *thought* it happened. Eve melted in his arms, molding herself against him for just an instant. But the moment was too soon gone and she regained her balance, straightening up and standing woodenly beside him. She was as close to him as she could possibly be without actually touching him. Only the hem of her diaphanous gown continued the connection.

Her gown and that damned honeysuckle scent.

****

There wasn't much room in the vestry. Such a tiny room would never hold the wedding party *and* the rather large person of the bishop. Hill preceded her into the room and Eve carefully picked her way along the uneven stone floor, standing as close to him as she dared.

Suddenly, someone behind her stumbled and pushed her into his arms. It was odd—there was never any doubt in her mind that Hill would catch her and keep her safe—just as he had on so many other occasions.

It had also been a cramped space when she and Hill hid from Monsieur Jones in that outer building at Terra Bella. Hill had held her so close that she could feel his hard muscles flexing along her back. He had one arm wrapped around her waist, holding her securely against him. His other hand, thank goodness, covered her mouth, preventing her from giving away their hiding place.

Eve closed her eyes and let the memories flash through her mind. For just a moment, it was summer again. As if her movement had triggered the same memory for Hill, she felt him slip an arm around her waist, steadying her, holding her close and, once again, keeping her safe. She was so tired of trying to make sense of how things had developed between them, so—for just that one moment—she relaxed against him and felt him hold her. She took a deep breath of the fresh balsam scent that she would always associate with the Duke of Camberton and, at least for a while, everything was as it should be.

But it was only a moment. Surely the sensation she had of him holding her so tightly was her imagination—coupled with fervent wishes. He was not hers—not anymore.

Maybe he never was.

The church bells began to ring and the wedding party followed the Duke and the new Duchess of Easton back into the church. The newly wed couple made their way down the center aisle, smiling and receiving felicitations from their family and guests. Without making eye contact, Hill offered his arm. Eve smiled at the congregation and accepted it without comment. Walking down the aisle together, they were once again cordial strangers.

Chapter 5

Outside the church, Avery and Linney were surrounded by a throng that had gathered in the street. Avery helped his new duchess into the magnificent carriage festooned with paper flowers and displaying the Easton family crest. After tucking in Linney's ermine lap robe, Avery followed her into the open carriage. The crowd swelled and roared its approval as the Duke of Easton began tossing gold coins to the children in the street.

With a start, Eve realized she was still holding on to Hill's arm. She dropped her gloved hand to her side as if she'd been burned and turned to face the man she'd tried so hard not to love.

They spoke at the same time.

"I expect I should—"

"That was a lovely—"

Luckily, no further conversation was necessary as guests spilled out from the church, widening the gap between the two and engulfing them with joyous greetings from family and friends. Eve fled to find the carriage that would transport her from the church to Haversham House for the rest of the wedding festivities and for a night of New Year's Eve celebrations.

"Eve! Eve, dear, over here!" Lady Ashby, Avery's Aunt Charlotte, waved her handkerchief and called out in a rather loud, exuberant voice.

Eve made her way to the smiling lady who looked uncannily like a ripe plum in her purple silk gown with the black soutache trim. Aunt Charlotte immediately linked her arm with Eve's, steering them both toward a waiting carriage. "I'm so glad you're riding with us out to Haversham House. The girls are beside themselves with excitement. Evidently red hair is the most fashionable color there is for hair at the moment, and the girls simply cannot wait to ask you all sorts of inappropriate questions about what it is that you do that results in such a brilliant color."

Eve smiled. A distraction would be most welcome—even if it was only to impart the disappointing news to the little girls that her hair color was natural and she did nothing to give it such a burnished copper color.

"I *told* Avery that having the breakfast all the way out at Haversham House would be a great inconvenience for everyone," continued Lady Ashby, settling back into the cushy carriage. "But you know Easton. He never was one to worry about inconveniencing anyone else. Nothing mattered except that he marry his Linney as soon as possible. I'm sure my Grandmother Ashby is already turning in her grave, what with having such an extravagant wedding before the full year of mourning is over for Avery's father. I can only image what the dear lady would say about a wedding breakfast being held so far away from the church!"

Eve opened her mouth to voice a reply, but Aunt Charlotte was talking again. "I will admit, however, that Lady Haversham's entertainments are always so enchanting and certainly well worth the trip. No one has more brilliant, more festive, more glittering celebrations.

She is, hands down, the most popular hostess in all of London and its surrounds, but as far as I can tell, this is only her second wedding. She hosted my other nephew's wedding to Lady Rowden at the end of last season, you know. The Duke of Whitley—Easton's brother—well, half-brother. Their mother was my sister, so they also share me as their aunt. Whit is quite a bit older than Avery—in fact he treats him like a younger brother. Hill too—that is, the Duke of Camberton. My word, that's a lot of dukes, isn't it? And then if you add in Edgewood, Whit's friend, who is the Duke of Marsden… Well, who knew so many dukes would be in the same place at the same time without someone being crowned!"

Eve smiled and nodded, realizing that Lady Ashby required no real response from her.

"Of course, Lord and Lady Haversham insisted on giving Linney and Avery the entire event as a gift. Isn't that lovely? And on New Year's Eve, no less. Well, it's certain to be the social event of both the new year *and* the old! Mark my words, people will be talking about this celebration for years to come—even those who have absolutely no connection to Easton and his new duchess."

Charlotte leaned over to whisper loudly to Eve, "I didn't think Vivian would attend, what with her confinement so close. It would never have happened in my day, mind you. But she promised Linney she would be here and so she was. They are first cousins, you know. Wasn't Linney's gown lovely? I don't know *how* her mother was able to create such a stunning design in only four short months—that's hardly enough time for anything." Charlotte paused her monologue to wave at another guest.

"And wasn't the Duke of Camberton looking well! At one point I thought that you and he—well, you know, would make a match of it—but it was obvious today that you were rather on the outs with each other. Nothing too serious, I hope. But it doesn't matter. The whole *ton* knows that he's set his cap for Nadine Bateman-Jones, Viscount Glenly's younger sister. Camberton has escorted her everywhere for the past several weeks. I wouldn't be surprised if they make an announcement soon. Lily! You and Rose stop tormenting Marguerite. Remember she gets ill riding in the middle. Rose, you and Lily must take turns at the window."

Sitting back against the plush velvet squabs, Eve reflected on how very long those four short months had been. Evidently four months was long enough to create a beautiful wedding gown. It was also long enough for the love of your life to completely forget about his promises to you.

Alas, it was nowhere near enough time for your heart to forget about him.

Chapter 6

The Duke of Whitley didn't know nearly enough about the man who had been Napoleon's spymaster and most trusted advisor, but everything he *did* know told him that the man was running rogue—he was unpredictable and erratic, making him even more of a threat than before.

For several weeks now, Whit had been receiving reports that, while Napoleon was safely ensconced under guard on his island prison of Saint Helena, Monsieur Jones was still fighting the war. His actions were those of a madman, and the man's brutality, not just to his enemies but also toward his own operatives, was well documented as cunning and consistently cruel.

The fact that Jones was English and of the aristocracy was as much a part of his mythos as his actual feats. He sometimes went by the name "The Frenchman," perhaps because of his penchant for the French garotte as his favored killing method, but more likely as a slap in the face to his fellow Englishmen. It was perhaps this aspect of the man that galled Whit the most, and the irony of the moniker taken by the traitorous Englishman was not wasted on him.

And now, Jones had started down a path of retribution that meant danger for Whit, for his lieutenants, and for anyone else associated with them. Unable to free his beloved Napoleon, Jones had started exacting his revenge on everyone who had participated in the emperor's downfall. He had vowed to make Whit and those working for him pay dearly. In Jones' unhinged mind, the Duke of Whitley, aided and abetted by Easton, Marsden, and Camberton, were to blame for his current circumstances and for Napoleon's defeat.

In other words, Jones was hunting dukes.

Whit's latest intelligence confirmed his suspicions that not only was the Frenchman planning the elimination of the four men whom he saw as instrumental to his downfall, but he had vowed to make the four pay more dearly by harming those whom they loved—specifically, the women they loved. If the information from Whit's contacts was accurate—and Whit had no reason to think it was not—Jones was not only hunting dukes, but he was also hunting their duchesses.

Whit would have preferred to leave his own duchess safely at home being pampered as her delicate condition required, but there was a part of him that was glad she had insisted on being here where he could keep an eye on her. Besides, there was no way that Vivian would have missed her Cousin Linney's nuptials. The two were more like sisters than cousins, and God help the man—or woman or even spymaster—who thought to come between them.

To date, the Frenchman had always made a sardonic point of inflicting equally brutal punishments on those who displeased him or who were expendable. But while the killings of men were usually quick, he took his time when murdering the women, often tormenting them by offering mercy—even freedom—if they would willingly have sexual relations with him. There had never been any eyewitnesses to any of this—just rumors and hearsay. Until now. This time they had a witness.

"You sent for me, your grace?"

Whit refocused his thoughts on the man striding up to him with two flutes of sparkling wine. He accepted one of the glasses and touched its rim to Camberton's. "To my brother and new sister-in-law!"

"To the bride and groom," responded Hill, draining the flute in one long draft. "I must admit that in all the years I've known Avery, I have never seen him so smitten—and that's saying a lot. There was a time there when he fell in love several times a day!"

Whit grimaced. "Yes, I remember it well." He shook his head. "I don't want to remember it, but I do. Those were the days when I felt that even being half-brothers with Avery was too close a connection. And, of course, you were right there cheering him on."

"Oh, come on, Whit. We weren't that bad, were we?"

Whit raised a single eyebrow and gave Hill the famous icy gaze that was known throughout the *ton*. Even after all the years he had known Whit and all the time they had worked together, Hill still found that gaze unsettling.

"Suffice it to say that those years represent events that have been carved indelibly into my brain, never to be erased." Whit took a deep breath and finished his wine. "What I wouldn't give for that to be my primary concern right now."

"You've had news?"

Whit nodded. "Yes, and so have you." He handed Hill an envelope addressed in a feminine hand. The seal had been broken.

"This came from Glenhaven. I took the liberty of opening it. Miss Bateman writes that her brother is coming home sooner than she expected and if you want to talk to him, you should travel to Glenhaven today."

Hill took the unfolded paper and skimmed the words, written in a flirty, feminine hand, as Whit continued.

"You'll recall when I sent for you at the end of the summer, I had only some whisperings to go on. Now I have significant evidence that this bizarre scheme is real and that Jones is either on his way back to England or already here. When he was occupying himself in France, I could be satisfied just tracking his movements, but now that he's in England, he has to be stopped. Unfortunately, since nobody knows for certain who the bloody lunatic is, tracking him lately has consisted of following the path of bodies he leaves behind."

Whit paused and shook his head. "And yet…I have this persistent feeling that the man is hiding in plain sight."

"Do we know where he is now?"

"Most of the reports indicate that he is back in England, although we don't know where. He was on the continent for several weeks. There were accounts that he tried to meet with Napoleon but was turned away. That may have been the last straw for him. His focus has changed from serving Napoleon to revenge, and he's eliminating anyone—friend or foe—who stands in his way. His ultimate goal is still unclear—I *thought* he was obsessed with killing Vivian and myself, which is why I wanted her close despite her condition. But this new information confirms that he's after you, Edgewood, and Avery as well."

Whit shifted as he continued to survey the area immediately surrounding their conversation. "He must realize that we're after him. Fortunately for us, he is such a narcissist that he can't imagine we will succeed in finding him. What progress have you made toward infiltrating Glenhaven?"

"As you can see from the letter, I have been successfully pursuing the Honorable Miss Nadine Bateman," said Hill. "She has given me permission to address her as Nadine, but it has taken me longer than I'd anticipated to convince her that I am interested in marriage and not the illicit liaisons she keeps proposing. I had to craft myself a new reputation as *besotted* rogue. I told her that I wanted to speak to her brother, but she kept making excuses about his whereabouts. She almost never talks about Glenly and when she does she appears to be afraid of him. Is he still the best link you have to Jones?"

"There were one or two indications that Jones might be Scottish, but they came to naught. Or, I should say, one of them came to naught. The other one led to Edgewood. I told him about it and he confessed to being Jones in his off hours." Whit smiled. "I told him to be careful. After his disappearance last year I strongly considered the possibility that he might have been turned. Thank God he was with me when Jones took Vivian. Otherwise I'd never be able to trust him."

Hill searched Whit's face for a sign that he was making a joke—a smile, a slight upturn of the great man's lips—but found none. This was the Ice Duke living up to his name. Hill and Avery had often tried to impress Avery's half-brother with their manly capabilities, and, in almost all cases, had received only a raised eyebrow for their troubles.

For his part, Whit was trying his best to think like a deranged killer. For all the years spent tracking Jones, all he really had to go on at the moment was contradicting intelligence that put Jones anywhere from Paris to Edinburgh. It was just this past summer when that had finally started to change.

As Napoleon grew weaker and weaker, his army started to look to their own sense of preservation. Jones had grown increasingly erratic, with no rhyme or reason to his movements. At the end of August they had a bit of luck: one of Monsieur Jones' expendable operatives didn't die. At least not right away.

It was a very sloppy mistake on the part of Jones—perhaps the result of pressure or haste—but it gave Whit information that he did not have before. Fortunately, the injured man knew he was dying and, like most of Jones' informants, had no allegiance to the madman. And so, for a very small sum that was to be sent to a family up north, the man uttered just two words when asked about the identity of Monsieur Jones: "Ask Glenly."

With the informant now dead, Whit needed more evidence about what role Glenly played. It was crucial that there be irrefutable evidence before he could even begin to accuse the head of one of England's oldest and most loyal families of being in league with Napoleon's spymaster. He'd called in Hill to find that evidence.

"When are you returning to Glenhaven?" Whit had never been good at social niceties or at covering his impatience.

"I planned to leave tomorrow, but with this latest news, I need to go now. When I told Nadine I wanted to speak to her brother after the new year, she invited me to

Glenhaven and assured me that his lordship would be in residence by Epiphany at the latest—evidently they have a longstanding tradition that brings all travelers home to observe the holiday as a family. My thought was to get there before Glenly, so I can search his private rooms. Once he arrives, I'll find a way to search his personal belongings for some connection with Jones."

"Once you meet with him—are you then engaged to his sister?"

Hill laughed. "That is a very sticky wicket. I'm hoping to get away with simply asking for permission to court her, but, if necessary, I will ask for her hand. And then, like the scoundrel I am, as soon as I collect the evidence you need, I'll tell Nadine that I have fallen in love with someone else and allow her to break off our engagement."

"Will playing the part of the dishonorable duke be a problem for you? You won't be able to tell anyone why you threw over the lady."

Hill shrugged. It was a fair question. "I have worked very hard over the past few months to build up my tarnished reputation. I have received multiple declarations of undying love, all of which I have callously rejected. Nadine will be no different."

Until quite recently, Camberton had one of the most dubious reputations in the ton. He had grown quite good at attracting the ladies—especially those who were irresistibly drawn to his wicked ways—and yet, when it came time for him to end a dalliance, he had, so far, managed to do so without making enemies. His method was to turn the lady down gently with the softest of rejections and allow the lady to jilt him. He then peppered the gossip rags with a healthy dose of self-recriminations that usually ended up making his victims feel sorry for *him*.

And for those few lucky ladies with whom Hill had actually engaged in affairs, the reports of his prowess as a creative, attentive, and masterful lover were part of his mystique that still served him well.

Of course, all of that changed the day he was kneed in the groin by a grubby Lady Eve in the barnyard of the Dog and Pony Inn. For some reason, since that day, he'd not been interested in other ladies just as he'd not been able to get the scent of honeysuckle and manure out of his mind.

Whit nodded. "As long as there is nothing to connect you to me, you should be fine. Just be careful with Glenly. He and Jones are connected, I'm sure of it. And Glenly is a very powerful man. He could accuse you of spying and shoot you himself and no one would question his actions. Or he could have his friend Jones kill you. Jones fancies the garrote, you know. Do you think the sister knows where Glenly is at the moment?"

"It's hard to tell, but I don't think so. Every time we met in London, she would always change the subject before I could learn anything. Truthfully, she's been more interested in setting up clandestine meetings and compromising positions for us—anything that would cement a marriage between us. She even suggested—more than once—that we take ourselves off to Gretna Green. Of course that would have spoiled my whole plan of getting into Glenhaven so I can search it. I think Nadine wants to present her brother with a *fait accompli*. Evidently she was betrothed to the Earl of Norwich when she was born, so his lordship is bound to put up a fight. But he's at least twenty-five years her senior, so Nadine has no qualms about breaking the betrothal to marry me. Her mother, the current Lady Glenly, was not as happy about the prospect of breaking the betrothal."

"Not even to add a duke to the family?"

Hill grinned. "Well, that helped, I must say. Once Nadine's mother realized that her daughter was sharpening her talons for a duke, she started having visions of presiding over the society wedding of the year."

"I'm afraid she'll have to compete with Lady Haversham on that front. When are you riding out?"

"After I speak to Avery." He grimaced. "I was supposed to open tonight's ball with Eve and the bride and groom. I need to let him know that I won't be there."

"Does that give you enough time?"

"It's hard to say for sure, since I don't know where Glenly is traveling from, but I'll make it work."

"And Hensen is going as your valet?"

Hill laughed. "He's not thrilled about it, but yes, he's agreed to accompany me. It was either him or Avery. And under the circumstances, I appealed to Hensen's sense of romance as well as to his sense of duty."

A loud boom from several strategically placed fireworks reminded Lady Haversham's guests that the evening festivities would be starting soon as the wedding celebration continued and the New Year's Eve fun began. Whit hurried off to find Vivian, leaving Hill to his preparations.

Watching Whit's swift progress to find his wife, Hill sighed. He had very much been looking forward to dancing with Eve to start the ball. After their brief encounter at the church, the idea of having her in his arms again made him catch his breath. He knew she was furious at him and he had some idea of how much he'd hurt her. But if he could finally unmask and capture Jones, then his mission would be complete and he could go to Eve and explain everything.

The sun would be setting soon and the fireworks would start after dark, with the ball to commence shortly after that. Hill sighed and then smiled a small smile. With any luck at all, by this time next year, he and Eve would be celebrating *their* marriage. Earlier today, he'd finally prevailed on Whit and received permission to tell Eve the very basics of his mission once he returned. He couldn't give her detailed explanations, of course, but at least after he returned from Glenhaven, he could find someplace private and tell her that his actions were not as they seemed. He could ask her to wait for him. And, if he had anything to say about it, he would steal a kiss from those soft lips that had haunted all of his dreams since the last time he'd kissed them at Terra Bella.

Chapter 7

August 1815, four months earlier

The relaxed, carefree days of late summer were an idyllic time at Terra Bella—a time full of laughter and love and friendship. Throughout August, the four friends spent almost all of their time together. Sometimes the gentlemen would ride out for a day of shooting, and on several occasions, Linney and Eve went to the nearest town to shop and have tea. They threw caution and propriety to the wind, rising before dawn to see showers of shooting stars or going swimming after sunset to find relief from the unusually warm temperatures. They gathered apples in the orchard, they learned to milk goats when Avery's goat herder was incapacitated for a few days, and they laughed so much that their cheeks ached. Almost every evening they dined together and the conversation was always lively.

Avery had an understanding with Hill that he wanted to spend as much time as possible alone with Linney. Being the good friend that he was, Hill did his best to suggest all sorts of outings and adventures that gave the two love birds numerous opportunities to be together.

"You do know that leaving them alone means that you and I are also alone?" Eve had pointed out the obvious to remind herself as much as to inform Hill.

"Linney is supposed to be *my* chaperone."

Hill had laughed and said that particular aspect of the situation was a bonus.

Considering the amount of teasing and good-natured squabbling that went on among them, it was amazing that Eve could remember only one serious disagreement she'd had with Hill the entire time—and she blushed to the tip of her widow's peak every time she thought about it.

It was their last outing of the summer. In just a few days, Hill would be returning to London, summoned back to work by the Duke of Whitley. Eve and Linney were leaving just a few days after that—Eve to her home at Tanglewood and Linney to London. The gentlemen had taken over managing every aspect of the day down to the very last detail. Cook had prepared a sumptuous lunch and Merton, the butler, had provided some of Terra Bella's finest wine. The outing was to be a complete surprise; Linney and Eve didn't even know their intended destination.

They four rode out early in the morning and the ladies were thrilled to learn they would be visiting the ruins of an old castle, the one-time home of one of Avery's ancestors. Although most of the buildings inside the castle's keep had been torn down and their materials reused elsewhere, three of the castle's turrets and the parapets that linked them were still standing strong. The spiral stairways to the top offered a challenging climb, but, according to Avery and Hill, also boasted an amazing view. They found the perfect place to picnic under an ancient weeping willow, on the bank of the river that had once been used as the castle's moat.

After lunch, Linney pled a headache, so while she

and Avery stayed on the blanket in the shaded seclusion of the willow tree, Eve and Hill decided to accept the challenge to climb to the top of the castle's towers. After a steep climb up an enclosed staircase, they finally came out into the sun onto the high walkway where ancient archers had defended the castle.

Eve tried waving and calling to Linney and Avery, but to no avail.

"Let them be," said Hill, grinning and grabbing her hand to lead her across the walkway and up the final steps to the top of the tower and its panoramic view.

"This is amazing!" gasped Eve. "It feels like you could see forever. If I owned this land, I would build a house here and put my bedroom in a tower so I could have this view through all the seasons and at all times of the day. Can you imagine watching the sunset from here? Or the moonrise?"

But Hill's idea of a perfect view was much closer. The vivid blue of the sky complimented Eve's fiery red hair and the vigorous climb had encouraged tendrils to escape the knot on top of her head and curl at the nape of her neck. Her cheeks were pink from the exercise and from her enthusiastic delight. When she smiled up at him with a twinkle in her gray eyes, Hill could hardly stand it.

He reached out and twined one curl around his finger. "Would I have to call to you to let down your hair so that I might climb up and rescue you?"

"You may climb up, your grace, but please don't take me away—stay up here and enjoy the view with me."

At that moment, Hill could think of absolutely nothing he'd rather do.

Looking for a way to distract himself from the powerful desire he was feeling, Hill turned away from Eve to regard the horizon. "You know, Avery punched me because I said I thought your hair was pretty."

"He did?" Eve was horrified. "Why on earth would he do that?"

"At the time I believe he had designs on you to be his future duchess." Hill laughed at the confused look on her face. "Of course we were only ten, so he may have changed his mind since then."

Eve laughed then. "Did you punch him back?"

"I should have, but he was the heir apparent and always got away with everything."

"I remember that visit," said Eve. "A snowstorm had made the roads impassable and my mother and father stopped at Terra Bella to seek shelter. Avery's mother was so beautiful. I remember thinking that she must be a princess."

"That's what I thought about you. You were about three and you were the first person I'd ever seen with red hair, although, if I recall, it was more golden then than it is now. I told Avery I thought your hair looked like a sunset and that's when he punched me."

Eve laughed. "Do you want to know a secret? I followed Avery around and even tried to kiss him once or twice because my mother told me to, but you were the one I really wanted to kiss. I was fascinated by you—maybe because you were tall and seemed so grown up."

Hill ignored the annoying voice in his head as he took the hand he'd been holding since they'd reached the top of the tower and pressed a kiss to its palm. He looked up at her and said gruffly, "I wonder if I might claim that kiss now."

With her other hand, Eve touched a finger to his lips, tracing the shape as her tongue nervously traced the line between her own.

That was all the invitation Hill needed. He pulled her gently into his arms and they were soon exploring each other with tender kisses and whispered endearments. When Eve put her head back to take a breath, Hill placed kisses on her throat and trailed them down to the top of her décolletage. Holding her with one hand, he moved the other down her arm and up her side, lightly brushing his thumb over her breast and smiling as he felt the tip harden beneath his touch. He gently cupped her breast and circled the rising peak with the tip of his finger. Rather than pull back at the increased intimacy, Eve melted into him. pressing both breasts against his hard chest as his hands continued their exploration of her waist, her hips, her bottom.

With each sigh and moan from Eve, Hill's passion grew. Pulling her tightly against him, he nibbled at her ear and kissed the soft spot at the base of her neck before returning to taste her lips again. He suckled gently on her bottom lip before taking her mouth, and when she tentatively touched her tongue to his, he deepened their kiss, his heart pounding and his body growing harder. He continued his quest over her body, running his hand up and down her thigh. He rucked up her skirt so he could find the bare skin above her stockings and caressed her there as she pressed harder against his growing arousal.

Eve was returning his kisses with the same passion he felt. He trailed his fingers up the inside of her thighs and found the mound of curls that hid her hot center. When he dipped his finger into the molten heat between her legs, she caught her breath. He stroked her intimately, first with one finger and then added another, caressing the sensitive folds again and again as he continued kissing her lips, her throat, and the tops of her breasts. When he gently touched the very center of her sex, he heard her gasp and felt her start to clench around his fingers as he kissed her gently toward the edge of a climax. Suddenly Eve shuddered. She moaned and called his name, and he could feel her tense as she reached the pinnacle of her passion. He pulled her against him and held her as she shuddered again and again, and then sank into his arms. For a little while they said nothing, the only sound their beating hearts, which eventually found the same rhythm.

After a few more minutes, Hill kissed the top of her head and put her away from him. He was hanging his head.

"Hill, that was… It felt wonderful. Is it always like that?" whispered Eve. Her eyes were shining and a flush still colored her skin. "I've never experienced anything so lovely."

"Eve, it was unforgivable of me to take advantage of you like that. I just… Are you all right? Do you want to sit down?"

Other than her somewhat shaky knees, Eve had never felt so wonderful in her life. She didn't want to do anything—except possibly more of what they had just done. Did that make her a wanton woman?

"I'm so sorry, Eve. Please accept my most sincere apologies. I was so caught up in the moment. We are friends and I took advantage of you."

Eve was quiet. He was sorry? Was he expressing regret for what just happened? She had been there too and was just as much to blame—if, in fact, there was a need for blame. What must Hill think of her?

"Hill, I…"

But he was talking again. "Please, Eve, you don't have to say anything. You have every right to be angry with me. I swear I didn't mean to use you so crudely. I can't believe I let my desires get the upper hand. I can promise you it won't happen again." His eyes never met hers. "We should return to the others now."

Hill went in front of her as they went back down the stairs. They reached the bottom without talking—the easy comradery of that morning now gone. When they reached the wide driveway, Hill offered Eve his arm and with only the most necessary of words spoken between them, they walked back across the bridge to the other side of the moat.

Chapter 8

Hill and Avery stayed long with their cigars and port that evening, and Linney, still suffering vestiges of her earlier headache, retired early. After finding a somewhat worn copy of Miss Austen's *Pride and Prejudice* in the library, Eve decided that she, too, would retire for the night.

She didn't see Hill again until the next afternoon when he sought her out and asked her to walk with him in the garden. She acquiesced eagerly, thinking that he was feeling better about their romantic interlude yesterday. Her mind raced ahead, happily anticipating more of the amazing kisses and caresses that still had her dancing inside and tingling down to her toes.

After seating Eve on a bench in the gazebo at the garden's far end, Hill very woodenly went down on one knee.

"Lady Genevieve, would you do me the very great honor of accepting my hand in marriage?"

The offer had all the romance of a judge issuing a death sentence.

Eve laughed delightedly. She assumed Hill was teasing her. Of *course*, she wanted to marry him, but not now, not yet. Trying to decide whether to reply with a dramatic refusal or a saucy acceptance, she suddenly realized Hill wasn't laughing.

Or even smiling.

"Hill, what is it? Has something happened? Why are you looking like that?"

"Looking like what?"

"Like you just lost your best friend."

Hill swallowed carefully. "I asked you a question, Eve."

"You're serious."

"Of course, I'm serious! What did you think? That this was some kind of pantomime? It is my responsibility to help you out of this predicament and my duty to offer you my hand in marriage, and I would appreciate an answer."

Eve furrowed her brow in confusion.

"Is there a problem with something I said?" asked Hill.

"No," said Eve. "Absolutely not. It was lovely. In fact, I think you should use it word-for-word on the next lady you offer for. Perhaps she will be more amenable to having you solve her—how did you phrase it? My *predicament*?"

Hill stood up from his proposal pose and turned away. He ran a hand through his close-cropped hair, making parts of it stand up straight. Eve fought an uncontrollable desire to laugh, but bit her lip as he turned back to face her.

"Eve, please. I know my duty. A man—a gentleman—doesn't do the things I did yesterday and then fail to offer marriage to the lady in question. I behaved in an unacceptable manner and have endangered your reputation. I'm trying to do the right thing. I've compromised you and I have a—"

"If you say 'duty' one more time, I will not be responsible for my actions. Why on earth would I want to marry you—or *anyone*—who proposed out of a sense of duty? I would rather be an old maid than marry a man who only saw me as a responsibility to be undertaken."

"It's better than being ruined."

"I don't think it would be."

"I can assure you, it is."

"*Can* you? Have *you* ever been told you must marry a man who sees you only as a 'predicament' to be remedied? Has someone told *you* that you can't possibly make any important decisions about your life simply because you're a woman? Have you ever been bartered over like some kind of livestock to be bred or faced with a *fait accompli* and given no choice but to marry a man who has already forced himself on you? Have you ever been told that your dreams are unimportant compared to the rules of society?"

"Actually, I have," said Hill, his eyes blazing. "You see, my lady, in the same way that a sullied reputation takes away *your* choices, it also takes away mine. I am expected to offer my hand in marriage to any woman who manages to get me alone long enough for her to cry foul. What's more, I am then classified as a rake simply because I tried to offer assistance to the lady. And as far as dreams are concerned? Well, all of mine took flight the day I was informed that I was the ninth Duke of Camberton. So don't you *dare* talk to me about having choices taken out of your hands."

Eve was quiet. He certainly presented another side of the picture—one that she had never thought about.

After a minute, Hill spoke softly. "Eve, if a man did to Henrianna what I did to you yesterday and didn't offer her marriage, I would call him out."

Eve scowled at him. "And from what you've told me

of Henrianna, I expect she would be as outraged as I if she were offered a proposal of marriage only out of duty. What's more, if you meddled in *her* business, she'd probably punch you!"

Eve stood up and put her hands on her hips. "Hill, I was there too. I *allowed* you to do the things you did. I *wanted* you to do them. I realize that they were things a lady probably isn't supposed to do or even know about, but it was wonderful! I do understand what you're saying, and I thank you for your kind offer. You may rest assured that you have honorably discharged your duty, your grace, but my answer is no."

"Eve, please." He was using that slow, placating voice again. "I don't think you fully understand how society can…show its displeasure with women—ladies—who engage in this…that kind of behavior."

"Are you truly saying that *I* don't understand how society can treat ladies who dare to behave differently? Or express an opinion not shared by their husbands?"

"That's not what I said…"

"That's exactly what you said."

Evidently Hill decided it was time to change tactics.

"We could make a trip up to Gretna Green tomorrow, if you like."

"Oh, good. So, you *are* interested in my opinion on the matter?"

"Of course, I am. Why would you think otherwise?"

"Perhaps because you seem to have thought all this out and decided what we should be doing without ever consulting me?"

"Is it because I didn't propose properly? I do beg your pardon, Eve. It was thoughtless of me to suggest that you would enter into marriage without a proper proposal. I don't have a ring, darling, but—"

"Hang the proposal and hang the ring!" Eve's gray eyes had gone dark with anger. She could feel the Irish temper that her mother always warned her about begin to rise. "And don't call me 'darling.' " She started to walk away but then turned and took a couple of steps back toward Hill.

"I am not a *predicament*, your grace. You have no duty or obligation toward me, and I do not need you—or anyone else—to take responsibility for me. And just to be crystal clear, I will *not* be going with you to Gretna Green—today or *ever*." Taking a breath, she shrugged and issued her best shot. "Besides, what we did yesterday was nothing *that* outrageous. I've had more sensual experiences with other men behind a potted palm, so you needn't worry about 'ruining' me. Certainly my past encounters didn't seem to bother *you*."

The hurt on his face showed that she'd hit her mark. Exactly as she wanted. She looked up at his agonized face and said stonily, "Again, thank you for your kind offer, your grace, but I must decline."

To be clear, Hill wasn't the first man she had kissed, but he was the first man who had… Well, the first man whom she had allowed to take her to the next level. And the one after that. She instinctively knew that they had gone right to the brink of no return. But they *had* stopped. Hill had insisted on it. Which was just one more reason why his proposal this morning was so insulting.

"Why are you being so pig-headed and stubborn about this?"

"Why are you being so arrogant and callous—by the way, not traits I'm looking for in a husband. Why are you insisting that you save me from ruin that exists only in your mind, your grace?"

"Eve!" Hill stood and looked at her with a scowl on his face.

"Yes, your grace?"

"Stop calling me 'your grace'!"

"Is that not the correct address for a gentlemen with your title?"

"That's not what I mean and you know it."

"I *thought* I knew several things about you, *your grace,* but obviously I was wrong."

Hill stopped pacing. "What the devil does that mean?"

"I don't know which of those words you're unable to understand, *your grace,* but I am happy to go over any of them that are troubling you."

"If you don't want to marry me, then just say so!"

"I believe I did."

"Very well, but don't come crying to me when you change your mind."

"I'm quite confident that you would be the very last person to whom I would appeal for help."

"Very well, Lady Eve. Good day." Hill stormed off down the garden path without looking back. Eve had never seen him so angry.

"And good day to you too, your grace," she called after him. "Oh, that man!" She angrily stomped her foot like a child.

The idea of going back up to the house right now was unthinkable. She couldn't return—at least not yet—so she started down a path that she vaguely remembered led down to the lake. It didn't really matter where it went as long as it went away from *him*. What an arrogant, condescending know-it-all! How dare he presume to know what was best for her? He had no standing to do that—he was not her brother or her father or anyone else with any say over her whatsoever. His idea that she was ruined was so smug and almost boastful. She was such a feeble-minded woman, that she was obviously unable to control herself when she was alone with him and had inevitably succumbed to his irresistible charms. How dimwitted did he think she was? Why did he have to make everything so difficult?

Her fury had propelled her all the way around the big lake and now she followed the path back up to the gazebo. Even after her long walk, she was still angry—no, she corrected herself, not angry. Scared. She had lashed out at Hill—not because she was angry with him for proposing to her, but because she was scared he didn't love her enough to marry her without being forced to propose. She was scared that he would find someone else to love more than her and scared that he would leave her—so scared that it made more sense to send him away rather than wait for the inevitable to happen. Maybe then it wouldn't hurt so much.

Eve sat down on the bench inside the gazebo and then slipped down to sit on the cool, stone floor. She was tired and sad and so disappointed, and she had no idea what to do now. How was she going to act the next time she saw him?

"I imagine that depends on how he acts when he sees me," she said to herself, wishing fervently that she could just turn into a butterfly and disappear.

She recalled the look in Hill's eyes. Like a trapped animal, she thought. How unfair—for both of us. The poor man was simply trying to do the right thing—at least his version of it. But wasn't that the problem? How would she ever know whether he actually loved her and wanted her? She didn't want to end up married to someone simply because he thought it was his responsibility to do so. She didn't want to be someone's duty to fulfill. Women did it all the time, she knew that. But could *she* live with that kind of love when she wanted so much more?

Eve lay down on the gazebo floor with her cheek on the cool, smooth stone, struggling to hold back her tears. It didn't matter now. Hill was gone and now she would never know.

Chapter 9

As Hill packed for his journey to London in that last week of August, everyone at Terra Bella—from the newest scullery maid to the Duke of Easton himself—breathed a sigh of relief.

Things between Camberton and Lady Eve had been uneasy for several days. The reason for the tension was something only those two knew—even Linney and Avery had heard only the barest of explanations. A casual observer might not have noticed much of a difference, but the mutual comradery and all the joy of a blissful summer was gone, replaced by cool courtesy and painfully awkward silences.

The night before Hill was to leave, Eve couldn't sleep. To be fair, she hadn't slept well either of the last two nights. Not since that ill-fated proposal and their quarrel. Since then, she and Hill had gone to great lengths to avoid each other and, when circumstances dictated that they be together, they had been polite, but little else. Nothing about what a future might hold for them. In fact, at the moment, they were barely speaking at all.

And, to make matters worse, she had picked a fight with him right before dinner.

And during dinner.

And after dinner.

All because he'd had the temerity to propose

marriage—which was really less of a proposal and more of an edict: "Your reputation will be ruined, so you should marry me."

One sentence and, in a matter of minutes, the dream she'd been dreaming all summer turned into a nightmare.

What would have happened if she'd taken the time to explain how his words sounded to her? Would he have said different words that were more to her liking? Were there words that would have made her fling her arms around his neck and say, "Yes" to his proposal with all her heart?

It was too late now.

The warm temperatures coupled with her overactive mind made sleep impossible. The heat had been intense all day and the setting of the sun brought only a slight reprieve. After hours of tossing and turning in her bed, Eve thought to escape the heat and the closeness of her room by walking along the lakeshore in hopes of finding some remnant of a cool breeze.

It was dark—even the moon was setting and leaving her. But, as if to offer her one last present, a shimmering moon path guided her to the edge of the lake.

Eve shivered in the heat. How in the world had things gotten to this point with Hill? They had quarreled before, but this time it was different. She had a bad feeling about it. "I don't think he's going to forgive me this time," she whispered to the moon as it finally slipped below the horizon. "And he's leaving tomorrow."

There was nothing else she could do. Even if she wanted to talk to him, she had no idea where he was. She thought briefly of going back up to the house and enlisting the help of a footman to find him, but it was late. Everyone was already in bed. Perhaps she could—

"Ow!"

"Oh, I do beg your pardon!" Eve had stumbled over a person lying on a blanket out under the moonless sky.

"Eve?"

Of course it would be Hill—who else?

"Eve, what are you doing here? It's late."

Eve blushed into the darkness and murmured an apology. She turned to leave but stopped when she heard him say, "I always look first for Orion's belt."

She paused and turned.

Hill continued. "When Henrianna and I were three years old, my father showed us the three bright stars in the constellation and told us it was our birthday gift. Every time I see it I think of him—and my sister."

"That's a wonderful story," said Eve. "I love that I can always find Orion quickly in the winter by the three stars in his belt."

"Do you have a favorite constellation?"

"Corona Borealis," said Eve promptly, forgetting herself and sitting down at the edge of the blanket with her knees pulled up under her voluminous nightgown. "So many of the stories my father told me when he was trying to teach me about the stars just didn't make sense to me. I remember thinking that the people who named the constellations must have been terrible artists! Or maybe they just had vivid imaginations. That's why I always liked Corona Borealis—it actually looks like a crown. But I also liked the plough and how you could use it to find the North Star." Eve laughed. "You know, even with the North Star, I always seem to get lost at night."

"No night sense," said Hill. "I have it in spades, so I'm never lost."

"Never? You've *never* been lost?"

"It's like a sixth sense. Both my sister and I have it. Ask anybody. Ask Avery. He hated that Hen and I always knew the right direction."

"Hen?"

"That's what Avery and I called her—she hated it almost as much as she hated 'Henrianna.' But maybe that's because Avery and I would tease her by making chicken noises when she tried to tag along with us."

"I remember how nice she was to me when my family visited Terra Bella. She's older, right?"

"Haven't I told you this? We're twins, but she was born first—twenty-two minutes earlier—something she never lets me forget."

"Where is she now? You never talk about her."

Hill went quiet. Eve could hear his measured breathing over the cacophony of tree frogs and night creatures. Finally he cleared his throat and said tightly, "She's in Paris."

"My goodness! Paris? How long has she been there? Wasn't she in danger from Napoleon's army? Is she there with her husband?"

"She's been there a couple of years, and from what I've been able to ascertain, she's not in any immediate danger." Hill paused for the briefest of moments. "As I understand it, she's the mistress of one of Napoleon's generals, so, no, she's not married. She's a French whore."

Eve was alarmed at the coldness in Hill's response. And the anger. After a moment or two of awkward silence, she started again. "I'm sorry. I didn't mean to…"

"It's not your fault," he said, sounding more like himself. "It's just…I don't like to talk about it."

This time the silence was more comfortable. After a few more moments, Hill resumed the conversation. "With the exception of Orion's belt, I've always liked the planets better than constellations. See that bright star there? That's Jupiter. I like that the planets move through the sky like the sun and moon. It gives you the feeling that life is going forward. The constellations seem like they never change."

"If you like planets because they move faster, then you must love shooting stars."

"I do. In fact, that's what I was hoping to see tonight when I came out. The Perseid meteor shower is supposed to be visible tonight and tomorrow night, but I've been watching for at least an hour and have only seen three."

"Three? Really? I don't think I've *ever* seen three shooting stars in one night. I've probably only seen three in my whole life!"

"I don't think I've ever known a woman who was so enthusiastic about the night sky. Why is that?"

"My father was a mapmaker, remember? He taught me all about celestial navigation. I can find the latitude and longitude of any position, but I don't seem to have any luck at seeing shooting stars."

"That's because you're sitting up. Your eyes can't see the sky as well when you have to keep turning your head and bending your neck like that. I promise if you lie down and watch the sky over the lake for ten minutes, you'll see a shooting star."

Eve laughed. "You promise? You're that certain of yourself?"

"I'm that certain of the Perseids. Look, there goes one! Too late—it's gone now. You really must lie down to see them."

"What happens if I don't see one in ten minutes?"

"Then I owe you a boon. You can ask for anything you'd like."

"And if I do see one?"

"Then you owe me."

"Done," said Eve, flinging herself down on her back with her head close to his. "But just so you know, I have no intention of staying out here all—oh, look!"

Hill chuckled. "That, madam, is what we call a shooting star and my win."

"Very well," sighed Eve. "It was worth it. What is your boon?"

"A kiss," he said.

Eve raised her head to look at him and then quickly delivered a peck on his cheek.

"No, no, no," said Hill, sitting up to protest. "That wasn't a kiss. That was just a buss. That was something you give to Great-Aunt Mathilda when she comes to visit."

Eve laughed. "I do beg your pardon, your grace, but my experience in kissing is somewhat limited. Perhaps you could provide some instruction?"

"What about all of that experience you've had behind the potted palms?"

Eve blushed, but thankfully it was too dark for Hill to see. "I may have exaggerated that particular circumstance somewhat."

Ever the opportunist, Hill leaned toward Eve and brushed his lips over hers, softly stroking their smoothness. He pressed gently and, trailing a finger down her cheek, he slowly traced the line between her lips with the tip of his tongue, urging them to part. When she kissed him back and parted her lips, he slipped his tongue in to find hers, waiting for her to object. And when she said nothing, he descended deeper into the kiss, increasing the pressure and demanding she reply. Much to his delight, she did.

Trying to find the perfect position, Eve melted into the kiss, wanting nothing but more. When she parted her lips and allowed his tongue entry, it set off frissons of pleasure in her breasts and deep in her core. Sensations that echoed those pleasurable moments in the castle ruins. She tentatively met his tongue with the tip of hers and received another shock of desire that made her shiver. She covered every part of his mouth with small tender kisses, dancing around his lips and his trimmed beard, as he growled his pleasure.

Breathless with desire, they finally parted. Hill exhaled deeply and lay down again flat on his back. Eve could hear his heavy breathing. After a minute, he raised his head to look at her and said, "Now *that*… That was a kiss. That's the kind of kiss you owe me."

He chuckled at her eyebrows raised in surprise at what he considered to be a clever ploy, but Eve was not to be outdone. Her eyes twinkled as she said, "Let me make sure I have this right."

This time it was she who pressed her lips against his, leaning over him and caressing the sides of his face with her fingers and then her palm. Bending over him, it was she who slid the tip of her tongue past his lips, exploring, searching, and sucking gently when his tongue tangled with hers. Breathing his breath even as she tried to catch her own. After a few more seconds, she pulled away.

"Was that satisfactory, your grace?"

"Yes…yes, I think that was exactly right. I think you've got it quite right, Lady Eve." Hill smiled up at her and then slowly drew her back down beside him on the blanket, holding her hand over his heart as she laid her head close to his for their own private viewing of heavenly bodies.

"There!" they cried together as a particularly fiery light streaked across the sky. And just like that he was kissing her again.

Softly at first, like the fog stealing across the lake, he gently brushed his lips over hers as he whispered her name coupled with every endearment. He leaned up on one elbow so he could see her in the starlight, toying with the tendrils of hair that had escaped her coiffure, and then he kissed her again. This kiss was more demanding and she reveled in it. Right now he seemed happy to accommodate her every emotion.

Hill kissed his way down her throat as she arched her back and gave more of herself to him. He trailed kisses down to the edge of her wrapper. and pulled it open. The fine lawn of her nightdress was transparent in the starlight and he could clearly see the darker areoles and pointed nipples and the shadowy depths between her legs.

Sitting back on his knees, he untied the satin ribbon that held her gown together and gently parted the lace edges.

"Will you let me touch you?" he murmured.

"Isn't that what you're doing now?"

"Yes, but there's so much more I can do if you will let me."

"Hill, I do want that, but isn't this what got us in trouble before? I don't want you to feel that you must ask me to marry me because we do that."

At first Hill was silent. Then he said, "How about

this: I rescind my previous offer of marriage and promise not to ask you again until after Avery and Linney's wedding, at which point I will have a proposal of marriage that will make your heart melt and have you throwing yourself in my arms."

Eve giggled. "That sounds perfect! But does that mean you will…that we can still…you know, tonight?"

Hill chuckled. When he spoke, his voice was low and full of desire. "That's up to you, my lady. I am at your service and more than happy to defer to your wishes on the subject."

"My wish is that you let me touch you, here…" Eve kissed him on the lips. "And here…" She kissed his chin. "And here." She kissed the curls in the vee of his open shirt and then proceeded to kiss her way downward. "And here. And then you kiss me wherever you want. Just remember that I've never…"

"I promise that you will still be a virgin, Eve. I can give you pleasure without taking that from you." He kissed her hard as he brushed a thumb over her breast and circled one tender tip.

She caught her breath at the sensation and he kissed his way down between her breasts, stopping to lave one taut peak and then gently blowing to watch them harden under his gaze. Eve's intake of breath at the sensation made him smile. He took the first hard point between his lips and suckled gently.

At Eve's sigh, he used his tongue to circle her nipple before sucking again. She arched her back and moaned when he stopped to move to her other breast where he repeated the slow tantalizing dance before continuing his journey. This time he trailed kisses over her belly and down to the soft curls between her legs.

Eve pulled her knees up and whispered his name. Hill moved back up to lie beside her, kissing her face and lips all over again. He sent his hand back down to her dark red curls and toyed with them as he stroked her soft folds. When he pressed that same finger into her wetness, he groaned. She froze.

"I promise, Eve. Trust me, " he whispered

And she did.

"You're so wet, my love," he whispered. "You like how I'm touching you, don't you?"

"Yes," she whispered back. "Yes, it feels so good. I've never felt anything like this before."

"Just wait…there's more."

His strokes grew more persistent, and he sent his finger into her wet center again, still moving, still slowly arousing her and taking her higher and higher.

"Hill, I'm…I'm not sure what I should do," she whispered.

"Don't worry. Just feel me touching and holding and kissing you. Let me help you find pleasure."

As he stroked his long finger in and out of her wetness and circled the tight, hard bud at her core, Eve moved her hips in the same rhythm, feeling the sensation of desire building and building, and taking her higher and higher until, at last, with a cry of surprise and release, she came apart. She shuddered as waves of pleasure washed over her and Hill held her tight in his arms.

****

The summer night had cooled at last, but there was nothing but heat between the two lovers. As he promised, Hill had kissed and stroked Eve and led her once again into that ancient rhythm as he teased her with the sensations of desire building, stopping, and then building again. When she came back to him, with a sigh and a final shudder, he kissed her nose and then her lips. "Did you enjoy that?" he murmured beside her ear.

"That was… Oh, Hill, it was amazing and felt so good. I had no idea it could be like that."

"I'm glad to hear you say that, my sweet. I love watching you come for me and feeling you shudder in my arms." He bent to whisper in her ear. "And I plan to be the only one with whom you ever share that pleasure."

Putting her hands on either side of his face, she pulled him toward her. "I promise," she said, smiling at the sudden scowl on his face and the fierceness in his eyes. "No one but you." She kissed his lips softly like a petal drifting on a breeze.

He raised up on one elbow as he cradled her beside him. "What am I going to do without you? I don't want to leave. You know that, don't you? You know that I love you, but I have to go back to London—Whit's message sounded urgent. I'll come and find you as soon as I can so we can talk and make plans. But for now just know how very much I love you."

"I'll miss you so much," she said, tears suddenly in her eyes. "Will you write to me?"

"Every day, if I can," he said, his finger tracing the trail made by one of those tears. "I promise."

"Hill?"

"Mmm?" He started to kiss the tears away.

"I love you too."

****

They parted the next day.

Eve kissed Hill goodbye in front of Linney and

Avery and the servants—actually he kissed her with a big sweeping, public kiss that left no doubt to anyone where things stood between them, and she kissed him back for so long that even Avery had to clear his throat to remind them where they were.

The servants cheered, Eve blushed a very becoming pink, and Hill rode off in a flourish. Eve waved her handkerchief—it was actually one he'd given her—until he rode around the bend and out of sight.

Try as she might, Eve could not help the tears that started. Linney tried to comfort her by telling her that it was just four short months until she would see him again—when they were all back together for the wedding. And in the meantime, offered Linney, there were letters.

Assuring her best friend that she would be fine, Eve wandered back down to the lake to remind herself of Hill's whispered words of love in their time together. Things would be better, she told herself sternly, when he sent his first letter. He'd promised to do so as soon as he arrived in London.

But no letters ever came.

If not for Linney, Eve might have worried that Hill had been injured or set upon by highwaymen. She answered her friend's cryptic inquiries about whether she had heard from Hill in the negative, desperately trying to save face by adding that they were just friends and she hadn't really expected to hear from him.

Whether Linney believed her or not was unclear, but Eve's words did pave the way for Linney to continue to send uncensored observations about Hill's outrageous behavior. Evidently he had been seen around London with a string of women—from actresses to widows. His reputation as a rake had died down while he was out of town, but now it grew more scandalous with each passing day. Eve remembered one particular letter from Linney that added a postscript saying that her maid had heard that the Duke of Camberton was characterizing his summer at Terra Bella as "an entertaining, but inconsequential summer."

At least she was glad to know she merited the status of being entertaining—even if it was inconsequential.

After Linney's last letter in late November, Eve slipped away to her father's tower study that the new Earl of Tangier had declined to use because of its many steps. Eve loved the view from the bank of windows that turned a rather mundane countryside into a breathtaking panorama. The wind whistled around and through the tower at this time of year, but it was just what Eve needed—a place where she could finally let her tears fall. Where she could finally give in to the gut-wrenching sobs that poured out from deep inside her soul.

These were the tears Eve refused to shed when she finally realized that no letters of love would be coming from Hill. These were the tears she wouldn't let fall when she read Linney's letter describing Hill's conquests around town and his seeming infatuation with Nadine Bateman-Jones. These were the tears she was determined to hide a month from now when she stood beside Hill at the front of St. George's Church to witness the happy-ever-after love story of her two best friends.

And when she'd finally, *finally* cried out all of those tears, Eve dried her eyes and resolved to start a new chapter in her life.

Chapter 10

Eve flew into her room at Haversham House as if demons were on her heels. She closed the door none too gently behind her and leaned against it for a minute to catch her breath.

Nancy, Eve's maid, looked up in surprise as her mistress fell into the room. "You gave me a start, Lady Eve," she scolded. "I was just going to have them come and take your trunks away. Everything is unpacked, and I'm going down now to press your gown for tonight." Nancy held up the pale green silk ballgown that had been exquisitely embroidered with white lilies of the valley at the hem and all over the bodice. Only a few wrinkles showed in the skirt.

"Pack everything up again," said Eve. "We're leaving." She crossed the room and sank into the overstuffed chair in front of the fire.

Nancy paused in mid-step and glared at her mistress. "Whatever are you talking about, my lady? I've only just got all your gowns fitting in the armoire—all except this one."

"I mean it. Stop right now and pack everything back up. I'll send for my trunks once I'm far enough away from here. Better yet, Mother can bring them with her when she returns home. I need to leave now."

"But I've just got everything put away," wailed Nancy, looking despondently around the tidy room.

"Well, you'll just have to pack everything up again. I'm not staying. I made my speech at the wedding breakfast, but I'm not staying for the ball. I can't. I just can't. I *won't*." Eve couldn't bear to see even one more minute of Hill cavorting with all the other female guests at the wedding. The man had the social awareness of a pig in slop.

"You won't what, milady?"

Eve's voice dropped off. Wasn't it enough that she'd had to walk down the aisle with the man, underscoring the irony of knowing it would be the only time they would ever walk down an aisle together? Wasn't it enough to be pressed up against him only to have him steady her by putting one arm around her waist and drawing her safely back against his hard, muscled chest—a chest that she knew from personal experience was covered with the softest dark brown curls that twisted around her fingers as she ran them over the warm, hard planes that—

"Never mind. We're leaving," repeated Eve, taking a deep breath and narrowing her eyes at Nancy, daring the maid to defy her edict. Running up the stairs had left her breathless—or was it the possibility of another close encounter with Hill?

"Are you certain, milady? Did your speech go well? I'm sorry I missed it." Nancy had played the part of attentive audience as Eve practiced the words that accompanied her wedding breakfast salute to the happy couple.

"I forgot most of it," said Eve. "I'm not even sure I said their names correctly." Unfortunately, just as she had been about to impress the gathered guests with her witty yet eloquent and heartfelt best wishes, a lady on the other side of Hill had leaned toward him to whisper in his ear, displaying an inordinate amount of bosom, a fact that Hill seemed to enjoy greatly. Then the lady had touched his arm and giggled—*giggled*—as she cooed, "Why, yes, your grace. Certainly, your grace! Oh, your grace!"

The whole scene made Eve want to throw her champagne into his smug face. Wouldn't that be a comeuppance for the great and mighty Duke of Camberton!

Somehow she had managed to keep from spilling the sparkling wine as she stumbled through her speech. She only wished she had spilled it all over his lap, which would surely be bulging with his—

"We need to leave now." Eve stood up.

"But what about the ball tonight?"

Eve raised her chin defiantly. "I'm not going. I'm not going to be part of the opening set with Linney and Avery, and I'm not going to laugh and smile and pretend that we are all such good friends when all I really want to do is step on his toes with my heels and slam my knee between his legs again."

"Whose legs, my lady?"

"Never mind. I'll help you. We can pack everything up and leave immediately for Tanglewood."

"But what about Miss Braddock—er…I mean her grace? Won't she be expecting her best friend and maid of honor at the ball?"

Guiltily, Eve sat back down in the chair. The very last thing she wanted to do was to cause Linney or Avery distress on this, their special day. But really…she just couldn't be here any longer.

"If the shoe was on the other foot, wouldn't you

notice if she weren't there for you?" Calmly folding a nightgown, Nancy moved closer to Eve. "There's an awful lot of people here who are strangers to her. Seems like she might be looking for a friendly face about now."

Eve sighed and put her head in her hands. Nancy was right. She couldn't just leave a terse note telling Linney of her plans. She'd promised to be here for her friend, but…

She stood and went to stand at the window that overlooked the hibernating gardens of Haversham House. All the flowers used today had been grown in the huge Haversham greenhouses—Lady Haversham's way of ensuring that she had flowers for all of her celebrations all year round.

"I just can't keep running into…"

Eve stopped abruptly. Chances were good that Nancy knew everything about her interactions with Hill, but it would never do to act as if he meant anything special to her—at least not anymore. "I'll go and talk to her grace." Eve stood up with resolve. "If she absolutely needs me at the ball, I'll stay. But start packing, because I know Linney will understand and we'll be on the road in no time." She glanced wistfully at the cakes and teapot on the tea table. "I don't suppose that tray has anything stronger than tea on it?"

As Nancy shook her head, Eve sighed deeply. She squared her shoulders and started for the door. Linney would understand. She had to.

Chapter 11

"Oh, Eve, it's you. Thank goodness!"

Struggling to undo the back hooks of her wedding dress, the new Duchess of Easton smiled over her shoulder as Eve entered the room. "I sent Mary for some pins. Can you help me with these hooks? I thought I would go ahead and change into my ballgown even though it's early still. Did you decide on the pale green silk or the ecru lace for this evening? Eve?"

When there was no response to her questions, Linney turned around to find her best friend standing against the closed door, her eyes filled with tears.

"Eve, what is it? What's wrong? Why are you crying?"

"I'm not crying," said Eve, roughly wiping her face with the back of her hand.

"Well, if you aren't now, you look as if you will be any minute. What's wrong? Did your mother do something again?"

After a very small pause, Eve took a step toward Linney and the stubborn hooks. As she undid the back of the bride's dress, she said, "Linney, would you be terribly upset if I did not attend the ball tonight?"

"Are you ill? Oh, Eve, I'm so sorry! Do you want me to call for a doctor? I can have Mary ring for Lady Haversham if you—"

"No! No, I'm not ill. I just…I need to leave. I need

to go now."

"Go? Go where? What are you talking about, Eve?"

"It's too hard, Linney. It's just too hard. I thought I could do it, but seeing him all dressed up in his formal attire… Smiling at him as if we were casual acquaintances—as if nothing had ever happened between us. I thought I could do it, truly I did. I thought I had my heart locked up tightly, safe from him, but I don't. When he takes my hand or I take his arm it's like a knife through my heart. I don't think I could stand being on the dance floor with him, opening the ball with you and Avery. Every minute he holds me in his arms or twirls me around, every time he smiles at me, I fall in love with him all over again—even though I know he doesn't love me. And…I just can't bear it anymore."

Linney pulled Eve to sit on the chaise longue, holding her friend's hands as Eve continued. "I'm so sorry, Linney. I wanted this to be a perfect day for you and Avery, and I've tried, but please don't make me do this. Please don't make me dance with Hill and pretend that my heart is not breaking."

"Of course you don't have to stay, darling." Linney pulled Eve into an embrace. "I'm so, so sorry, Eve. Did he say anything to you? About why he…why he did what he did?"

Eve sat up, trying to laugh through her tears. "You mean did he say why he totally abandoned me the day after he practically proposed to me? Did he say why he never said another word to me until we met at the front of the church in the middle of your wedding? No, he didn't. He hasn't offered the first word of explanation."

That was just *one* of the mysteries that surrounded Hill's exit from Terra Bella. Avery claimed to know no more than Eve and Linney, but Eve was certain he knew more about Hill's sudden summons to London than he let on. And then there was Hill's re-emergence into London society as a dashing rogue at the height of the Season, creating even more questions—as had his surprise infatuation with Miss Nadine Bateman.

"I know I should despise him. I've *tried* to despise him, but I just can't. I can't, and it hurts so much to watch him pretend that we have no history. To see him with other women, flirting and stealing kisses from them the way he did with me."

Eve took the handkerchief from Linney and dabbed at her eyes. "I know he's always been a rogue and this behavior is *de rigueur* for him. I knew when he first touched me in the barn and I… Well, you know. I know I should be angry with him and treat him like the scoundrel he is, but when we met today, he kissed my hand and looked at me the way he looked at me when we were at Terra Bella, and—just for a moment—it was like it was this summer."

Linney's sigh brought Eve back to the present.

"I wish I had answers for you," her friend said. "Or, failing that, I wish I could knee him in the family jewels for you. Honestly, I was as shocked as you when you said you'd heard nothing from Hill. I admit I only had eyes for Avery, but even so, it was clear that you and Hill were… Avery said it too. He's known Hill since they were boys and he said he'd never seen him so smitten—that was his word, 'smitten.' So it wasn't just you."

Eve took a deep breath, willing the tears to wait for just a bit longer. It was good to hear that she was not the only one who had been taken in by Hill's attentiveness. She'd replayed every interaction between them over and over in her head, trying to find some explanation for his behavior—she was too forward, she was too inexperienced, she was too short, she was too plump, her hair was too red—but every time she came up empty. Certainly any of those things might be a problem for a gentleman, but they were all things that had been part of who she was from the start and Hill seemed to have gotten past them all. What had changed between them? She was so tired of going over everything. If only she could make her heart and head forget about him the way he had obviously forgotten about her. Seeing him this morning had opened the wound all over again.

"Do you understand why I have to go, Linney?" Eve's voice was just a whisper now.

Linney hugged her tightly. "Of course, I do. I know it was hard to stand up for us with him at St. George's and I love you for doing it. And your toast at the breakfast was perfect. I have to admit that a part of me was hoping that when Hill saw you again…"

Linney's voice trailed off and the two friends sat together, saying nothing. There was nothing more to be said.

Linney broke the silence. "Will you go back to Tanglewood?" The Earl of Tangier's family home was a day's ride from Haversham House.

"Yes, I think so. At least for a day or two. I haven't decided for how long yet. I want to go up to Blackwood and work on my father's map, so I may just keep going north after a quick stop. The only thing I know for certain is that I need to leave here today. I suppose I have to talk to Mother and see if she wants to stay or if she's going to—"

"Eve, I need to tell you something before you go."

Linney stood up and turned away from her friend. "I was hoping to save it for another time, but since you're leaving today, I need to tell you now. You need to know." She turned back to face Eve.

"Linney, what is it? Is it Avery?"

"No, no. It's nothing to do with us—it's about you. About your mother. It's something I should have told you sooner, but I know how much you've missed your father, and then with Hill being so awful…"

"Linney, you're rambling. What is it? What should you have told me?"

"I didn't want to give you something else to worry about. I haven't told anybody, not even Avery. I tried to—"

"Linney! Just tell me."

"Very well." Sitting back down on the bed, Linney took both of Eve's hands in hers. "Do you remember when we first went to Terra Bella to find the Easton engagement ring, and I went into the passageway while you went to your mother's room?"

"Yes. I was supposed to lure Mother out of her room so that you could search for the ring."

"Well, when I was in the passageway, I reached your mother's room before you knocked on her door. She wasn't alone. She was talking to someone. A man."

"Yes, I know. Avery and Hill said it was Monsieur Jones—the man they call the Frenchman. He's Napoleon's spymaster. We saw him come out of the passageway while we were waiting for you. That's when Avery charged in after you. Hill told me that Jones was an extremely dangerous man." She shook her head. "What has this to do with me?"

"While I was waiting for you to knock, I could hear

your mother talking to Monsieur Jones. She was… Well, she sounded like she was flirting, and then they were talking about you. Your mother said something about trying to make it look as if Avery had 'compromised my Eve.' And then Monsieur Jones said, 'You mean *our* Eve, don't you?' And your mother said, 'Yes, yes, of course. *Our* Eve.' "

Eve furrowed her forehead. "I don't understand. What are you saying?"

"I'm saying that I think Monsieur Jones and your mother have known each other for a long time. I think they were friends—actually more than friends. From what I heard, it sounded like they once—maybe still—had a…a romantic connection."

"A romantic… Wait, are you saying that Monsieur Jones and my mother were lovers? That's ridiculous. My mother would never…" Eve's protest faded. In fact, it would not surprise her at all to learn that her mother had been unfaithful to her father and had many affairs.

"That's not my point," said Linney. "What I'm saying is that Monsieur Jones sounded as if he were reminding your mother of something he knew about *you*. Eve, I think he was saying that he was your father."

"My *father*? You're saying that the man the entire British army is looking for, the man who has been labeled a traitor to his country, that man is my *father*?"

"I think so. I don't know for certain, but I thought you should know what I heard. I don't know what else he could have been talking about, but maybe I misunderstood. But, Eve, if he *is* your father, then you could be in a lot of danger. I overheard Avery and Whit talking about Monsieur Jones, and when I asked them if they were talking about the same man who had been at

Terra Bella, they said yes. They said that he's become even more erratic and more dangerous. They wouldn't say anything else in front of me, but Eve, if Jones is in contact with your mother, and if he is—or thinks he is—your father, then—"

Eve stood up abruptly. "I need to talk to my mother. I can't believe she would keep something like this from me. My father—my real father, Lord Tangier—always treated me as his beloved daughter. He left all his money to me—everything that wasn't entailed—not to my mother, but to *me*."

"I know. And I know how much you loved him, Eve. You talk about him all the time and I know you must miss him terribly. That's why I didn't want to tell you sooner about—well, about what I heard."

"I don't… Oh, God, Linney. What if Lord Tangier *wasn't* my real father? What if that horrible Jones person is my father?"

"Listen to me, Eve. Lord Tangier was your father in every way that counts. He was legally married to your mother when you were born. That makes him your father in anyone's eyes. He raised you and loved you, and you loved him. Nothing anyone can say will change that. I only told you this because I wanted you to know that Jones might pose a threat to you and I wanted you to be aware of that possibility. And truthfully, it doesn't really matter whether Jones is your father or not. If he *thinks* he is—if your mother told him he is—then you're still in danger."

Eve squeezed her friend's hands as she stood. "Thank you for telling me this, Linney. I know it wasn't easy." She kissed Linney on the cheek. "Have a wonderful evening and a lovely ball tonight. And at midnight, give Avery a kiss from me. I can't think of a better way to start the new year than with a new husband who loves you as much as Avery loves you." Eve pulled Linney into a quick hug and whispered, "Happy New Year, my dearest friend."

And then, before the tears started again, Eve hurried out of the room to find her mother.

Chapter 12

"I'm dreadfully sorry to do this to you, old man, but I have to go. Right now. I won't be here to open the ball with you and Linney. And Eve. There's no time. Whit just got word that Jones is back in England. I need to get to Glenhaven tonight so I can search as much of the place as possible before the viscount returns. Nadine's message said he was due back on the second or third of the month. Will Linney be very upset?"

"Don't you mean will Eve be very upset? Linney will be fine. She understands. But I saw how you were looking at Eve. Have you talked to Whit about explaining some of this to her? Surely keeping it all a secret puts her more at risk."

"I did ask him, and he agreed that Eve should know. Just her association with all of us puts her in danger. But it will have to wait until I get back. I don't have time to find her before I leave. I hate to ask this, Ave. I know it's your wedding night, but could you talk to her for me? Tell her I will explain everything when I get back, and maybe put in a good word for me? Tell her I'll be back as soon as I possibly can."

"Unless, of course, you get engaged to Nadine before then," observed Avery wryly.

Hill grimaced. "Well, sure. Like you do." He shook his head. "It's a lot, isn't it? Do you think she'll believe you?"

"In her present state of anger, I'd say the chances of her listening to you are almost zero—and may actually be in negative territory. I, on the other hand, am the bridegroom who has done the respectable, right, and most romantic thing. I have married my true love—and incidentally Eve's best friend—in a wedding for the ages, with festivities that will go on for days. I have vowed my troth to my beloved and have given her new jewels. In short, I am everything any woman could want in a man, so chances are good that Eve will believe anything I tell her—even if it's about you."

"You're insufferable when you're happy. If you weren't my best friend, I'd punch you right in the gob and wipe that grin off your fat mug."

Avery laughed. "I'm afraid that wouldn't help your chances with Eve at all, my dear fellow. Just leave everything to me. I'll tell Eve all the best things about you—if I can think of one or two—and make a case for your devotion to king and country above all things. By the time I finish spinning my tale, she'll be counting the hours until your return. Maybe waiting for you in that exquisite gown she was wearing when she walked down the aisle with you. The one that showed off her splendid figure and caused you considerable discomfort."

"Bloody hell, Avery! You're a married man. You shouldn't be noticing Eve's figure!" Hill was practically growling at his friend.

"I didn't, you idiot. I just wanted to get a rise out of you. Serves you right for misbehaving at my wedding and distracting me when I was trying to drink in the beauty of my lovely bride."

"She *was* beautiful," agreed Hill too quickly. "I've never seen such elegant wedding clothes. And the way it was cut so low to accent her—"

"If you want to live, my friend, do not finish that sentence." Now Avery was the one with sparks in his eyes.

"Ha!" said Hill. "What's sauce for the goose is sauce for the gander. How does it feel, having another man ogle your wife?"

"It's not the same. Linney is my wife in *fact*. At the moment, Eve is not even speaking to you."

"A matter of time, my friend. All a matter of time." Both men chuckled as they shook hands.

"Seriously, Ave. Thank you. And congratulations. I wish all the best for you and Linney." He pulled Avery into an embrace and pounded him on the back before letting him go. "And thank you for talking to Eve for me. Please tell her I love her and that I'll be back as soon as I can."

Chapter 13

Lady Tangier was resting when Eve burst into her room.

"For goodness' sake, Eve. Must you make so much noise? I had only just closed my eyes."

"Do. Not. Lie to me, Mother," said Eve, her quiet voice alarmingly at odds with the anger on her face. "Was Lord Tangier my father?"

Lady Tangier sat up slowly, removing a masque of steeped green tea leaves as she turned to face her daughter.

"Darling, whatever are you talking about? And why have you come storming into my room without even the courtesy of knocking? Honestly, Eve, I don't know what comes over you sometimes. You would think you had never been taught how to—"

"Tell me the truth," said Eve between clenched teeth. "Was Lord Tangier my father?"

Lady Tangier's wide, deceptively innocent eyes looked even bigger with her subtle application of kohl and a turban wrapped protectively around her unnaturally dark hair. "Eve, darling, do stop scowling. You'll give yourself lines and no one will ever want to marry you. Sit down and let me ring for some tea. You've obviously upset yourself and—"

"I don't want tea, Mother. I want the truth and I want it now. Was Lord Tangier my father?"

"Don't be silly, Eve, of course he was your father. He doted on you from the day you were born, spoiling you horribly. He was such a fool when it came to you. Why else would he leave his estate to you and not to me?" Lady Tangier's mouth hardened as she forced a smile.

"Someone overheard your little tête-à-tête with Monsieur Jones at Terra Bella this summer, Mother. So tell me, did you betray your husband and have an affair with that monster? Were you and he lovers? Is Monsieur Jones my father?"

"Oh, Eve, what utter nonsense. Whoever told you that was obviously mistaken and just wanted to upset you, dear. You should not believe everything you hear. You know how much your father loved you."

"I *do* know how much he loved me and I loved him," said Eve, "but that doesn't answer my question. Is Monsieur Jones my father?"

"I have never been so insulted in my life," snapped Lady Tangier standing abruptly and pulling her quilted silk robe around her. "How dare you stand there and insinuate that I—"

"Stop," said Eve. "Just stop talking and look at me, Mother. Answer my question. Is Monsieur Jones my father?"

Suddenly Lady Tangier's face crumpled, and she threw herself back down on the chaise longue. "Oh, Eve darling, it's not what you think," she cried. "It was horrible. The man was a guest of your father's. He attended our wedding and stayed at the house, and he…he seduced me on my wedding night."

Clutching a lace-trimmed handkerchief, Lady Tangier sat up. Tears threatened to mar her deftly applied paints, so she contented herself with sniffing pathetically as she continued her tragic tale. "At our wedding dinner, he was very attentive to me. All evening he was making inappropriate remarks, and he took every opportunity to kiss my hand or 'kiss the bride for luck.' At the same time, he kept pressing spirits and champagne on Lord Tangier until he was quite tipsy. I had never seen him so intoxicated—he was barely able to stand when I left to prepare for our wedding night. I waited hours for Lord Tangier to come to my bed, but when he finally stumbled into my room to exercise his husbandly rights, he was unable to… That is, he could not even… perform…the way a bridegroom is supposed to perform. He fell asleep on the bed and never even touched me."

Lady Tangier stood up and walked away from Eve. "In truth, I was relieved. I decided to go for a walk in the garden, and that's where Monsieur Jones found me. At first he was flattering and sympathetic and very attentive, but then he grew more and more aggressive. I quickly found out that he was not even French but was part of the English aristocracy. His told me his business was in France and much of it was secretive, so he often used a false identity."

With her back to Eve, Lady Tangier continued the story. "You are a young girl, Eve, and you should not even be exposed to these things, but the man seduced me and made me do vulgar, unspeakable things to him. In the end, he took my virginity as if *he* were my new husband. He told me to pretend that my husband had performed the deed on our wedding night and warned that he would expose me if I refused. He even cut his hand to smear a bit of blood on the sheets so that it looked as though Lord Tangier had consummated the marriage.

Then he insisted I get back in bed with my unconscious husband. I did as he demanded, and two months later I realized I was with child. Since Lord Tangier still had not bedded me, I knew the baby was not his."

Lady Tangier looked at Eve. "Of course, that baby was you. When I told Lord Tangier that I was expecting and that the baby had been conceived on our wedding night, he believed me and he was ecstatic. He loved you before you were born and for the rest of his life. No one could have been more of a father to you, Eve, so, tell me…how should I answer your question?"

Lady Tangier sniffed and looked at Eve with just a slight tremor of a smile. "He bought you a pony the day you were born. Did you know that?"

"Star," said Eve without thinking. "I loved that pony. She was so beautiful."

"He did his best to spoil you rotten. If it hadn't been for myself and Agnes, who knows how you would have turned out. I thought he would burst his buttons with pride at your coming-out ball."

Eve was smiling now. She remembered how her mother had scolded her father, who seemed determined not to let any of the eligible young gentlemen dance with her at her own party.

"I told him that it would not do to have you be a wallflower at your own coming-out party, so then he went and found the most charming, the most eligible, the handsomest young men and commanded them to ask you to dance. That entire Season was nothing but one young buck after another trying to win your heart, when I could have told any of them that your heart belonged to your father. I'm just glad you had at least that one year out in society before we had to go into mourning." Lady

Tangier dabbed at her eyes again.

Eve was quiet for a minute, remembering the times before her father died—for her mother was right. No matter what anyone said, Lord Tangier was her father. She adored him and he thought the sun rose and set in his only child, even though—or perhaps because—she was a girl. He'd taken her everywhere with him and, as a result, she became fascinated by his work as a mapmaker. As cartographer to the king, Lord Tangier had traveled the world, but most of the time he worked close to home so that his beloved daughter could accompany him on his various expeditions to survey and measure and create a variety of maps of the United Kingdom.

At an early age, Eve knew more math and could calculate complex equations better than most male students twice her age at university. What started as her father's desire to have Eve's company on his trips soon became a helpful association between a mentor and his apprentice. As Eve learned the skills and the art of making maps, Lord Tangier grew to depend on her abilities as his trusted assistant. At the time of his death, he was in the process of finishing his last commission for the King—a modern map of the British Isles that featured a level of detail never seen before. Going through Lord Tangier's papers after his untimely death, Eve found that the project was even more complete than she'd first thought. Then and there she vowed to finish the map on her father's behalf, as a tribute to him.

"Did my father—Lord Tangier—ever know? For once in your life, Mother, please tell the truth."

"Of course he never knew." Her mother's silken voice soothed Eve. "There was absolutely no reason for him to know. Under British law, he is legally your father because he is the man I was married to when I had you. And in case you are wondering, I never saw Monsieur Jones again until that day at Terra Bella."

Eve's world tilted once again as she watched her mother sit down in front of her dressing table, lying outright as she looked at herself in the mirror. Linney had just told Eve that she'd overheard Jones speak of visiting her mother often. It was as if her mother was incapable of telling the truth. Who knew what else she was lying about?

Lady Tangier leaned forward to peer more closely at her face in the mirror. "I was shocked when he appeared at Terra Bella that day. Shocked!"

"Was trying to get Avery to marry me your idea, or was that something Monsieur Jones told you to do?"

"Darling, I told you I never saw him again until that day at Terra Bella. You never listen to me!"

Chiding herself for being surprised that her mother lied as easily as buttering toast, Eve sighed. She would never be able to trust the woman entirely, but she knew her mother had spoken the truth when she said that Lord Tangier had loved his daughter more than life itself. So, let her mother have her secrets. What difference did it make?

"Now, Eve dear, shouldn't you be getting ready for the ball? With Linney married, you are the only unmarried young lady among your friends. This may be your last chance to find a husband, so you should look your best." Lady Tangier leaned forward, patting her cheeks. "You don't want to be an old maid, do you?" The lady sighed. "If only the new Lord Tangier were here tonight to see you in all your wedding finery, then you might be able to extract an offer of marriage from him. It's such a shame that you and Camberton have had a falling out. I had hoped… Well, I suppose that's water under the bridge. Which gown did you decide on for tonight, dear? Did you do as I told you and have Nancy lower the neckline on the green silk? You know how it shows off your bosom, and men do so love to look at ladies' breasts." Lady Tangier sat up straighter exposing and admiring her own well-endowed figure.

"I'm not going to the ball," said Eve, starting for the door. "I'm going back to Tanglewood tonight, and then I'm traveling up to Blackwood Abbey to finish Father's last map."

"I don't find your sense of humor very funny, Eve." Lady Tangier glared at her daughter in the mirror. "Whatever are you on about? You know you're to open the ball with Avery and Linney and Camberton. Have you forgotten? And you should mind your p's and q's while doing so, so that all the other eligible gentlemen will see you. Maybe *that* will make Camberton change his tune."

"I told you, I'm not going to the ball. I'm leaving as soon as Nancy finishes the packing. I came to see if you wanted to leave with me, but I've changed my mind. I don't want you to go with me. Enjoy the ball."

At the door, Eve paused and turned back to her mother. "One more thing, Mother. I don't know what makes you incapable of telling the truth, but I am finished listening to your lies. I know that Monsieur Jones visited you more than once. I know that you and he were and probably are still lovers. And even though I seriously doubt everything you just said, I do know one thing that's true. My real father was Lord Tangier and he *did* love me, and I loved him. And now I am going to finish the work he was doing for His Majesty."

"But what about me? If you take the carriage, how will I get home?"

"I'm only taking the carriage as far as Tanglewood. I'll send it back to collect you. I'm sure the new Lord Tangier won't mind. And, if he does, perhaps you could just show him more of your bosom."

Eve closed the door softly behind her and leaned back against it. It was a lot to take in, and yet she had never felt so free in her life. Or so sure of what she needed to do next.

****

A few hours later, Avery knocked on his wife's door—his *wife!* He'd expected to see Eve helping Linney get dressed for the evening, but instead her maid was doing her hair.

"Do you know where Eve is? I have a message for her." Catching Linney's eye in the mirror, he smiled a private smile that was just for her.

Eyes sparkling, Linney turned her head and frowned at him. "I knew it! You've already grown tired of me, haven't you? It hasn't even been a full day yet, and here you are seeking out other women." She sighed deeply.

With an almost imperceptible movement of his chin, Avery dismissed the maid and moved to stand behind his wife. Bending to kiss the bare nape of her neck, he whispered, "Never, my love." He moved his kisses along to the place where her graceful neck met her shoulder and their eyes met in the mirror. "You are the only one for me, and I will never grow tired of you—of kissing you, of touching you, of making love to you."

Linney sighed as she closed her eyes and sank back against him. The view that her low-cut gown presented was a vision he would take with him to the grave.

"Do you promise? For ever and ever?" Linney sat up to hear his declaration again.

Continuing his journey, he carefully placed another kiss on her bare shoulder and smiled as he watched the flush that spread across her bosom and up to her cheeks. "Always, my love," he whispered in her ear. "For ever and ever and then some."

"Why did you need to talk to Eve?" asked Linney, rubbing against him in a most suggestive way.

"Hill wants me to tell her that he loves her."

"What?" Linney sat up and turned toward Avery. "He wants you to what?"

"Tell her that he loves her and will be back as soon as he can so that he can tell her so himself. Turn back around. I want you to watch me make love to you."

"Where is he…ah…where is he now?" said Linney, her attention distracted as her body responded to Avery's wandering hands moving downward to cup her breasts.

"Where is who?" growled Avery, not wanting to take his focus off his wife for even a second.

"Hill," breathed Linney, fast losing the battle for coherence. "Where is Hill now?"

"He's gone on a mission for Whit, but he will be back soon." Avery's fingers had found the tips of her breasts and Linney gasped her pleasure.

"When…when he…when he…"

"When he does what, my love?" whispered Avery softly in her ear.

With a shudder, Linney did her best to focus. "What I'm trying to say is that when he comes back, he'll just have to leave again. Eve has left. She's gone home to Tanglewood—and it's all because of him."

"Well, then, I guess there's nothing else for me to do if she's not here."

"Should you send him a…uh…a note? A note to tell him that Eve's not here. Otherwise, he…uh…he won't even know where she is."

"I expect he'll do whatever it takes to find her," said Avery, resuming his determined exploration of his wife's décolletage. "I know I would."

Chapter 14

The trip was blessedly uneventful.

At Tanglewood, Eve traded Lord Tangier's carriage for a smaller, less conspicuous conveyance and fresh horses and traded her beautiful evening gowns for a much more practical wardrobe of men's shirts and breeches, a buckskin jacket, and sturdy boots—similar to the clothing she wore when she'd gone on expeditions with her father. The men's attire was magnitudes more comfortable, with none of the confining foundation garments that ladies were obligated to wear. As much as she loved wearing the bright silks, lush satins, and exquisite brocades, the men's garments that she'd had altered to fit her petite figure gave her the freedom she craved—and needed—as she continued her father's work.

At the last minute, Eve also brought her father's old greatcoat that she'd had cut down to fit her. She could still smell the pipe tobacco he sometimes smoked when he was out surveying the countryside and, in a small way, it was as if he were with her on this last journey to finish his map.

After two long days of travel, Eve, Nancy, and Ned, a footman from Tanglewood, arrived at the Three Crowns Inn in Blackberg, the tiny town just south of Blackwood Abbey, the vast estate belonging to the Earl of Tangier. As her father had done so many times before,

Eve took a room at the inn for the first night, looking forward to the tradition of ordering the landlady's famous pasties with the crust in the form of a crown.

As tenants of Blackwood Abbey, Nancy's family lived and worked on a farm just outside the village and, for generations, had been in service to the Earl of Tangier and his family. Eve gave Nancy leave to spend the evening with her mother, father, and her many siblings after extracting a promise from the girl that she would be back early to help Eve buy supplies and pack for her trek into the heart of Tangier lands.

Both Nancy and Ned Footman had offered to go with Eve on her journey into the wilderness, but Eve refused. This was a trip she needed to make alone, and not even the gentle scolding of Nancy's mother could sway her decision.

"I'll stay at the gamekeeper's cottage near the edge of the forest and be back in a fortnight," Eve said firmly. "If I'm not back by then, feel free to send out a search party to find me." She smiled at the concern on Mrs. Findlay's face and gave her a quick hug.

"Besides," she whispered into the good lady's ear, "you'll have your hands full getting to know Nancy's new beau." She laughed at the surprise on the older woman's face and then nodded solemnly. "I think this one might be serious." Eve smiled again as Mrs. Findlay looked around to pinpoint Ned's location and almost laughed at the sparkle in the woman's eye upon seeing her daughter deep in conversation with the handsome footman.

By midmorning the next day, Eve had collected and packed everything she needed for her two-week sojourn. Nancy and all her family waved goodbye as Eve and Ned rode out to the cliffs outside town where the familiar trail started. Agreeing to meet Eve back at the same place in just two weeks, Ned took her mare back to Blackwood Abbey as Eve started down the path that wandered in and out of the forest at the ocean's edge and eventually led to the gamekeeper's cottage.

Eve reached the cliffs that were the westernmost boundary for Blackwood Abbey lands by early afternoon. And, as she had done many times before, she stopped to admire the breathtaking beauty that surrounded her—the cliffs running down the coast in front of her, the thick, evergreen forest to her left, and, to her right, just beyond the breakers, the peaceful blue of the Atlantic Ocean. Drinking deeply from the bottle of water she carried with her, Eve let the anger and frustration of the past few days fly away with the brisk breeze blowing in from the sea.

The guillemots and storm petrels floated on the water, waiting for a chance at dinner, while the gulls floated on the wind, flapping their wings only occasionally as they made their rounds. Out where the waves were calm, Eve could see a school of porpoises breaching one after another in their own aquatic version of follow-the-leader. She let herself be drawn into the beauty and serenity of the moment, breathing deeply and raising her face to the warm sun. She couldn't help but wonder why her father had left this small stretch of coastline until the very end of his project. Maybe it was his idea of coming full circle. Perhaps he had decided that, because he knew every mile of it as well as he knew the back of his hand, it would be a satisfying way to end the mammoth project. Finishing the work in his stead felt right.

Eve didn't linger long. The gamekeeper's cottage was still several miles ahead and she wanted to get there before dark, which, in winter, came early this far north. At the cottage, she would set up housekeeping for her two-week stay. A pang of sadness went through her as she acknowledged that this was the first time she had stayed at the cottage without her father. She missed him, but walking down the path she'd traveled so often in his shadow made her feel close to him again. Nothing she had learned in the past few days could change her love for him and his love for her.

Eve could hardly remember a time when her father had *not* been working on this particular map. He'd shown her what he called his "tables of truth"—columns and columns of numbers that told the latitude and longitude for all kinds of landmarks and structures, from the highest mountain in the British Isles to the northern corner of the Tower of London. This was the information he used as the basis for creating his maps. He shared numbers and information with colleagues who were employed in similar cartographic pursuits and he often used measurements provided by area residents or local officials. Some of the numbers he used were from the work of cartographers as far back as Ptolemy in the second century, but by far, the most critical information was found painstakingly recorded in his bound leather books—the result of measurements he had taken himself, using his own tools, on his own expeditions.

Over time, Eve had become almost as competent with her father's instruments as he was himself. She clearly recalled the proud day when her father gave her a compass of her very own. It was styled like a pocket watch with a cover that flipped up when you pushed a button. She always carried it with her and it was still one of her most prized possessions. Engraved on the back of the compass were the words, "A compass points direction, but follow your heart to love."

As a child, she remembered reading those words over and over and begging her father to explain what they meant. He would smile and tell her that someday she would understand and, hopefully heed the wise words, even though he had not. Now, in her twenty-first year, she was beginning to understand what the passage meant and why it always made her father sad. Eve wondered if she would ever be able to "follow her heart to love"—especially after this summer. It seemed that the only thing *her* heart knew was how to fall in love with the wrong person. If only she had ignored her heart. Perhaps then she might have seen some warning signs about Hill and realized he was still a rogue—just like his reputation and everyone else told her he was. If she had ignored her heart and listened to them, she might have seen him for the toad that he was—a man who, for a whole summer, pretended that she was the light of his life.

In truth, the only thing she had learned from her heart was how it felt to be broken.

****

The sun was just slipping below the horizon when Eve spotted the gamekeeper's cottage ahead. Its wooded location gave it protection from the wind and storms, but it was still close enough to the cliffs to have a view of the ocean.

The breathtaking vista in front of Eve lifted her spirits and she was determined to push away the thoughts swirling around and around in her head like the waves pounding the shore below. She wanted to forget about Hill and all the rumors and gossip about him that had made their way to Tanglewood throughout the fall, and she was determined to forget about this most recent encounter with him at Linney and Avery's wedding. He had made it more than clear that he was not the man she thought him to be and that he was not in love with her. It was time for her to move on.

It was time for her to forget Hill and how he flirted with all the ladies—even the wallflowers. It was time to forget how his eyes crinkled at the edges when he grinned, and how his contagious laugh brought a smile to everyone who heard it. It was time to forget how, even though he towered above her, he always bent close to make sure he heard what she said. And it was way past time to forget his teasing demands and his brash declarations of love…and the sweet words that he'd whispered to her when they had kissed at Terra Bella. She had to forget everything because it meant the world to her—and it meant nothing at all to Hill.

The only problem was that to forget, she first had to remember.

Chapter 15

Hill's hurried ride to Glenhaven was grueling, but he wanted to make sure he arrived well before the family and guests gathered in the parlor to await the dinner gong. With Hensen's help, Hill bathed, shaved, and dressed in record time. He had just finished searching the elegant but somewhat shabby parlor where he was told everyone gathered before dinner when the first guests—Lord and Lady Dunham—entered.

On his previous visit to Glenhaven, Hill had noticed a dearth of servants. At the time, he'd assumed the help had been stretched thin because of the holiday season, but now it was clear that Glenhaven was being maintained with only a skeleton staff. Could it be that the family coffers had been depleted by helping to finance Napoleon's failed war?

The fields and tenant farms leading up to Glenhaven were in a sad state of disrepair and neglect. According to Whit, Glenly had recently sold off several of his holdings farther north. The family estate at Glenhaven was entailed with the title and so could offer little in terms of available funds and thus amenities—which might explain why Nadine had taken so long to invite him to visit. Certainly there was no lack of enthusiasm on her part, but perhaps she was unwilling for him to see just how financially strapped her family was.

It might also explain why the family was so willing

to break off a longstanding betrothal to Lord Norwich, their neighbor with whom Glenhaven shared a common border. Norwich was a friend of the last Lord Glenly and the betrothal had been arranged right after Nadine was born. But Norwich could not possibly compare his fortune—or his good looks and social standing—with that of the Duke of Camberton.

Nadine had managed to delay any wedding to Lord Norwich while she flirted—and by most accounts didn't stop at just flirting—her way through the *ton* in search of a more appealing situation. One hoped Lord Norwich was not expecting his bride to wear white, if and when a wedding ever did take place.

Hill quickly disguised his covert search of the room by welcoming his fellow guests. "I've helped myself to a sherry," he said after introductions were made. "May I pour one for you, Lady Dunham? I'm sure the family will be down any minute."

"How are you acquainted with the family, your grace, if I might inquire?" Lord Dunham accepted a glass of sherry from Hill for his wife and took one for himself.

"I am—shall we say—getting better acquainted with Miss Bateman-Jones," said Hill. "And you, my lord? What is your relationship?"

"The late viscount and I were at school together," replied Lord Dunham. "Our families have been friends for generations. Lady Dunham is godmother to the current viscount."

"So you know Lord Glenly well, then," said Hill, pouring another glass of sherry for himself.

"As well as anyone, I'd say. Although I've not seen the lad—"

"He's not a lad any more, my lord." Lady Dunham

frowned at her husband.

"You're right, as always, my dear." Lord Dunham lowered his voice in case the walls were listening. "Young Glenly has been involved in some hush-hush business for the King. Explains all that blasted business when he was home from university. From what I've heard, his lordship has turned out to be a great asset to the Crown."

As someone who actually *had* been doing the King's work for several years, Hill knew for a fact that Glenly had not. It was interesting that this was the cover the viscount had put about to explain his frequent absences.

"Surely that's all water under the bridge now?" Hill stepped closer to Lord Dunham to invite his confidences. Exactly to what "blasted business" was his lordship referring?

"Quite so," said Dunham. "But it was a scandal at the time. His own father found the letters. Someone as bold as brass had put them in with the post to be franked and the handwriting looked exactly like the young master's. They questioned the entire staff, of course, and a parlor maid claimed to have seen him putting the letters in with the others."

"He denied any knowledge of the letters," said Lady Dunham quickly.

"Of course he did," continued Lord Dunham. "And sure enough, the next day that same maid was found hanging from an eave in the barn. She left a note saying that she had accused him because he wouldn't pay her any attention. Seems she had developed something of an infatuation for the boy, and she was furious when he didn't return her regard. How could he? He was the heir and she was the daughter of a blacksmith. Of course, she did the right thing at the end and admitted her lies."

"What was it that the girl's father kept bringing up?" mused Lady Dunham, wrinkling her brow.

"Some rubbish about the girl not being able to write much beyond her name so how could she have penned such a long note. Dixon, the local coroner, paid no attention to that and closed the case quickly. After it was all over, young Glenly refused to speak to anyone about the girl. Said he wouldn't speak ill of the dead. Admirable, if you ask me." Lord Dunham took a sip of sherry before continuing.

"Tragically, the viscount died only a few days later. It was a senseless riding accident—saddle strap broke on a jump. Young Glenly was the one who found him. Everyone was in shock. The viscount had always been so fond of riding—he was the best horseman I knew. He was also a devoted royalist. The saddest part was that he never learned about the things his son had done for the Crown in the fight against Napoleon. Some of that information is still coming out. Perhaps now that the Corsican has been banished to Saint Helena, he'll be home more often. It's been his mother, the viscountess, who has kept the home fires burning."

"Glynnis did say that his lordship will be joining the party tomorrow, though," chimed in Lady Dunham. "It will be lovely to see him after all this time!"

So, Glenly would be back tomorrow. That left only tonight for Hill to find any evidence tying his host to Jones.

"Camberton?"

Lord Dunham's question caught Hill off guard. "I beg your pardon, my lord. What was the question?"

"I asked how you came to find yourself here. Isn't a

house party rather out of character for you? From what I've heard, this is a rather tame group for you to infiltrate."

Dunham's choice of words startled Hill. Had the man seen him searching the drawing room?

Lady Dunham tittered after taking a sip of sherry. "Oh, darling, you make him sound like one of Napoleon's spies. Perhaps his grace is here looking for a respite from all the *ton*'s fawning over him. Although I *have* heard that you had your eye on a widow from Sussex—at least that's the story *she's* telling. I believe some of the other ladies have other versions. But then that's to be expected when you consider all his wealth and talents." Lady Dunham lowered her lashes and looked slyly at Hill. "Everything *I've* heard about his grace points to his being quite the talented gentleman—*very* talented according to some of the ladies."

"Surely you don't put stock in the gossip of widows and old ladies, Lady Dunham." Nadine came up behind Hill and put a hand possessively on his arm as she pecked him on the cheek. "His grace is here because I asked him to come. He's sort of a late Christmas present…for me," Nadine looked pointedly at Lady Dunham and then turned to Hill.

"Pour me a sherry, won't you, darling? When did you arrive?"

The room was beginning to fill with family and guests—twenty-four in all—but no Lord Glenly. And no time to do any more reconnaissance. After dinner, and after the ladies had retired to the parlor for tea and the men had drunk their brandy and smoked their cigars, games were started in the parlor. At half-past two, Hill, with two other gentlemen, finally climbed the stairs to the guest wing. He and several others had just finished a nightcap in the library, allowing him a chance to study the lay of the land.

The closed door at the far end of the room obviously led to the viscount's private study. It was the most likely place to find any incriminating evidence to link Glenly to the Frenchman simply because it was the most secure. Hill had watched servants and guests all evening, but no one had opened that door. The question now was whether the door was locked, in addition to being off limits. Certainly if *he* had hosted such a large party of guests and strangers, he would have locked his study—even if it contained nothing more than personal correspondence and papers relating to the estate and even though doing so went against every known rule of hospitality. Perhaps Glenly was more trusting than he was.

He'd soon find out.

Upon retiring to his room, Hill listened to hear the other two guests enter their own rooms. He changed out of his evening attire into less conspicuous riding clothes and then waited for thirty minutes more. When he heard the clock in the downstairs hallway strike three o'clock, he opened his door and looked up and down the hallway. Shuttering the dark lantern he'd lit from the fire, he crept out of his room and worked his way back down the stairs.

The almost-full moon provided plenty of light through the windows in the great hallway. Hill tried to stay in the shadows as he made his way down the hall to Glenly's study and tried the door. Locked! Just as he'd expected. Picking up his lantern, Hill moved into the library. If he was going to have to pick a lock, he'd rather do it from the library side than from the hallway in plain view of anyone who happened to walk by. He tried the library door to the study, but it too was locked. He set the lantern on the floor and pulled a set of lock picks from his pocket. As he crouched in front of the lock, he heard a noise in the hallway. Had he been followed? Was Glenly home already? He stood up as the library door opened. A flood of relief went through him when he heard a sultry voice whisper his name.

Quickly he moved toward the ghostly white figure. "Nadine! What are you doing up? You must be freezing."

As Nadine stepped into the moonlight, he could see that she wore a diaphanous robe that seemed to float around her. The thin garment appeared translucent, outlining her slim figure and leaving absolutely nothing to the imagination.

"I *thought* that was you moving so quietly through the hallway," she purred putting her arms around his neck and rubbing herself against him. "I *had* hoped you were on your way to my room, but it seems you prefer old books. Or perhaps you were on your way to a rendezvous with someone else?"

Disentangling himself from her arms, Hill took a step back and laughed. "Of course not, my dear. I merely wanted a book to help me go to sleep. But how did you see me when you were all the way in the family wing?"

Nadine's laugh was low and as smooth as cream. "I wasn't in the family wing, darling, I was on my way to see you! I couldn't sleep for thinking about how it would be with you," she said. "So, I went to find you in your room and saw you going down the stairs." Standing on tiptoe, she pressed herself up against him again and whispered in his ear, "Would you like to see what I was going to show you, my darling?" Before Hill could say anything, Nadine stepped back and untied the gossamer robe, letting it float to the floor and leaving her completely bare before him.

No one could blame Hill for being aroused by the vision in front of him. Nadine was certainly a beautiful woman, and, as parts of his body would attest, he was a man who had been without a woman for a very long time. But after his initial reaction to Nadine's naked offering, his overwhelming desire was more about self-preservation than satisfaction.

"Nadine, you mustn't be here with me. And certainly not like that! You'll catch your death of cold. Now put your robe on and go back to bed before anyone finds you here and we are forced to marry immediately."

"I don't care if they do, darling. In fact, that's exactly what I want, don't you?"

Hill's mind was racing. "But do you really want the scandal? Do you really want to miss out on having a big wedding at St. George's, presided over by the bishop—a wedding that's attended by the entire *ton*? And a wedding breakfast that's so lavish you'll be the talk of the town for years to come?"

He could almost see the wheels turning in her head.

"If we are found together, then there will be nothing but scandal and disgrace. The old guard will gossip behind your back even if they smile to your face. There will be no society wedding with flocks of bridesmaids, and no beautiful gown for you to wear. The wedding will be a small, private affair—no guests or family—with the local vicar presiding. Or worse, over the anvil at Gretna Green. Is that what you want?"

Taking a step back, Nadine shivered and considered his words as he picked up her robe and held it for her to put on.

A soft knock at the closed library door and the door was opened by Hensen, who never batted an eye at Nadine's rather advanced state of undress. "Pardon me, your grace, but did you want me to bring that nightcap up to your room?"

"I'll see to it, Hensen. Lady Nadine just stopped by to wish me a good night. Would you light her up to her room? I will have finished my brandy and be ready to retire by then."

"Certainly, your grace." Hensen held open the door for Nadine to proceed him into the hallway.

The door clicked closed and—after pouring himself a brandy for his nerves and his story—Hill immediately returned to his work. Luckily, Glenly's caution only went so far. The lock on the door was of poor quality and opened easily under Hill's expert manipulation. *The things one learns at school*, he thought to himself. Only a few seconds later, he slipped into Glenly's study, quietly closing the door to the library behind him.

He had to work fast. He had no idea when Glenly would arrive or if—God forbid—Nadine should decide to seek him out again. He opened the lantern's door, letting a small beam of light into the dark room, and groaned inwardly as he looked around. What a mess! Stacks of paper were everywhere. If they had been less even, he would have thought the room had already been searched, or more precisely, ransacked.

Closer examination showed that the papers and ledger books and—was that a sketch pad?—everything else had been neatly stacked in piles. Was this some sort of technique for hiding information? Surely one wouldn't leave damning evidence just lying about. Only a madman—Hill stopped, remembering Whit's description of Jones as a man who was well over the edge of sane behavior. Glenly might well be on that same trajectory. Hill sighed and started looking through the papers on the desk. He didn't have much time. Glenly was due to arrive later today.

Most of the entries in the ledgers were related to travel. Did Glenly pay for Jones's travel? What else had he financed for the traitor? Bills, receipts, and other information about an estate in the north of England were in stacks on the floor in front of the enormous desk that dominated one whole end of the room. Perhaps this was about the land that Glenly recently sold. Stacks in a chair between the floor-to-ceiling windows revealed tenant records dated years ago—before Glenly had even inherited the title—along with receipts from what looked to be Nadine's coming-out ball just two seasons ago.

Sitting down at the desk, Hill leafed through the stacks on the desk. Oddly enough, the desk drawers were completely empty—except the bottom right-hand drawer, which held a box containing two dueling pistols. Hill closed the drawer and then froze as he heard footsteps in the hallway. He grabbed the lantern and shuttered the light, crouching behind the desk just as a key turned in the lock of the hallway door. He heard voices, but couldn't understand anything until the door opened.

"—can bloody well wait until after my bath. Is it ready?"

Hill was not a small man. The huge desk would hide him from someone at the doorway, but provided absolutely no cover from someone who entered the room and walked anywhere else. Preparing to defend himself,

Hill crouched a little tighter and dared not breath. At least he had surprise on his side.

"Then wake them!" The man's voice sounded furious. "And send Eversby to help me out of these clothes!"

The sound of a bag or bundle hitting the floor near the door startled Hill and he cracked his head against the underside of the desk. Biting his tongue to stop any sound, he held his breath. Had the man heard him? Hopefully the sound of hitting his head was drowned out by the door closing. Hill heard the key turn in the lock and then heard heavy footsteps going back down the hall. The house seemed to be waking up early to accommodate its newly arrived master.

Exhaling, Hill unfolded himself from his hiding place and went to examine the bag that had so purposely been locked in Glenly's study. He set the lantern down on the floor and let as much light through as he dared. In the small beam he opened the heavy leather saddle bag, rifling through the contents. He found a sheaf of folded papers stuffed into an inside pocket. The top paper was a list of some sort. He brought the page right up against the lantern so he could read it. The first item on the list was "Ice Duke." The next was actually two names: "Edgewood" and then "Marsden?" The third item was "Easton." The fourth name on the list was his.

Whit had said that Jones was hunting dukes. Glenly must be helping him. This was the evidence they'd been looking for—the connection between Glenly and Jones. He looked at the next page.

At first he thought it was a copy of the same list, but when he pulled the paper closer to the light he saw that this list contained additional names beside each man's name. A shiver went down his spine when he saw what had been added.

Jones and Glenly weren't just hunting dukes, they were hunting duchesses.

Beside the Ice Duke was simply "the codemaker"; beside Avery's name was "Linea Braddock"; beside Marsden's name was "Rose du Bois" and underneath that, two other names. Beside his own name was the name of a lady he had been seeing as part of his secret mission this past fall—before he met Nadine. He looked closer and saw that a line was drawn through that name. His blood ran cold when he saw the name that had been penciled in:

"Eve."

Whit had warned that Jones was planning to exact his revenge on the Ice Duke's lieutenants by going after their women, and this was proof. Not only was Glenly helping Jones, but Glenly himself was a danger to the dukes and their ladies.

Hill had to get out of there. He had to get this information back to Whit immediately—perhaps they could figure out a way to make Glenly turn on Jones. Perhaps they could appeal to Glenly's love of country or concern for his family. But whether or not that happened, the most important thing for him now was to find Eve and protect her. He should never have left her, but at least at Haversham House she was surrounded by friends and people who could keep her safe.

Hill glanced at the bottom of the paper and saw a drawing—perhaps a map? Below the sketch was a string of numbers. They meant nothing to Hill, but maybe one of Whit's codebreakers could tell if they were important. It was impossible to make out what the drawing showed.

Perhaps a crossing from France? Or maybe a rendezvous point? Whit said they thought Jones had most likely already crossed into England, but they had lost the trail soon thereafter. But why would Glenly have a map of Jones' route? Were the two planning to meet? Jones was on a killing spree—systematically eliminating anyone who had worked for him or anyone who could identify him. Whit's operatives had reported finding a number of bodies in France—some with their throats slit and some just garroted—strangled to death. Evidently, Jones' preferred methods of eliminating loose ends were fast, effective, and quiet. Would Jones spare the man who had financed and supported his futile mission? Or was Glenly also in danger from Jones? Perhaps that was why the viscount seemed so frantic?

Hill dug deeper into the bag to see if he could find something—anything—that would give him more information about Glenly's plans or Jones's whereabouts. Cravats, handkerchiefs, shirts, stockings—all seemed innocently stuffed into the bag until… Hill suddenly realized that the items of clothing were being used as wrapping to hide something more sinister. Slowly he unwound a cravat and stared at the dagger in a thick leather sheath. He pulled a shirt out from the bottom of the bag and a length of strong, flexible wire with wooden handles at each end fell out: a garrote.

Hill looked at the weapons he held in his hands and everything became clear: Glenly wasn't *supporting* Jones—Glenly *was* Jones!

He had to get this evidence to Whit. Folding the pages and tucking them into his shirt, Hill stuffed the weapons and other items back into the bag. It would be dawn soon. He had to come up with a plan that would let him leave Glenhaven immediately. Some kind of emergency that would allow him to leave before breakfast. He left the study just as he'd found it—only the bag at the door was missing two critical pieces of information. Retracing his steps back into the library, Hill remembered at the last minute to drink the brandy he'd poured, leaving the empty evidence of his nighttime wanderings. He opened the door to the hallway and ran smack into a man standing just outside. The frown lines on the man's face were deep, as if frowning was his usual demeanor. He was slightly shorter than Hill and dressed for travel.

"I do beg your pardon," said Hill, staggering back as he bowed and tried to appear overly intoxicated. "Just finishin' up a nightcap or two. His lordship's brandy's outstandin'."

"And who might you be," said the man, his eyes darting to the lantern Hill carried.

"Clever device, innit?" Hill held the lantern up, demonstrating the little door, then whispered, "Didn't want to disturb the guests nor none of the family. Which one are you?"

"Family." The word had never been spoken with more steel and ice. "I am Lord Glenly. And you are…?"

"I am drunk, Lord Lengly. I am most drunker than I should be…or meant to be. I had two, no…six, no…maybe eight brandies, and I'm afraid…I drank 'em too fast, my lor'," said Hill. He lowered his voice. "I was trying to forget a certain lady, but it is not working 'cause I still remembered her. I cannot stop thinking about my Elise. *Für Elise*, that's me. But Elise says she loves another who is not me." Hill let out a soft belch. "So now I have to find 'nother one—someone with as nice a dowry—and 's nice backside 's 'lise. That Miss Baitnum-Jones—Nadine—would do if she weren't besotted with that Camberton bastard. She's always been so…'commodating—you know whatta mean?" Hill bent toward Lord Glenly to whisper his next words. "An' she's got a fine arse. Do you know Nadine?"

Before Glenly could say another word, Hensen appeared at Hill's elbow. "Let me help you up the stairs, my lord. You should have let me bring the brandy to your room."

He turned to the man who was watching them closely. "I do apologize, Lord Glenly. His lordship doesn't hold his spirits very well."

"You're his valet?"

"I am, my lord. Hensen, my lord."

"Well, Hensen, I suggest that you take his lordship up to his room before he says something that cannot be made right and before I demand satisfaction for his speaking of my sister while he is in his cups."

"Yes, my lord."

With Hill's arm around his neck, Hensen half carried, half dragged him to the staircase "Watch the step, my lord."

Leaning heavily on Hensen's arm, Hill staggered down the hall under Lord Glenly's stoney stare with the evidence that Jones and Glenly were the same man plastered against his fast-beating heart.

Only when they reached the hallway to the guest rooms did Hill straighten up and clap Hensen on the back. "Well done! Thank you, Henson. You make an outstanding valet. Now pack up. We've got to leave. Now."

Chapter 16

Last night had been full of dreams—no, nightmares. All about Hill.

They all started the same way—with her in Hill's arms and him kissing her as if he couldn't stop, while telling her over and over how much he loved her. Then the dream changed to her walking down the aisle to meet him on their wedding day, until all of a sudden she was the bridesmaid again and Hill was marrying someone else who was walking behind her.

In another dream, she was standing alone at a ball while she watched Hill dance by with one beautiful lady after another.

The worst dream of all was where she watched Hill being stalked by a faceless man. The man chased Hill everywhere he went and finally cornered him in a dark hallway. In her dream, Eve tried to call out a warning, but Hill couldn't hear her. The man pulled out a knife and started stabbing Hill over and over. Then she saw Hill lying on the ground, bleeding, and the man had turned to come after her.

Eve woke to the sound of her own screams echoing in the small cottage. Shaking, she got up and wrapped a blanket around herself. She stirred up the coals from last night's fire and sat in a big chair that she pulled close to the hearth, grateful for the light and grateful for a reprieve from her dreams. Tucking her feet up under her, she closed her eyes and tried to sleep—at least for a few more minutes. The next time she woke, the sun was up and well above the horizon. She stood, stiff from her night in the chair, and put the kettle on to boil. Maybe once she started her work this feeling of despair from last night's dreams would go away. It had seemed so real. She wondered where Hill was now.

With new determination, Eve set out to accomplish as much as possible before the sun set. Her destination was a rocky outcropping of land that was the last landmark her father had referenced in his notebook and the point farthest from the cabin. The day was cold and crisp as if winter were trying to be on its best behavior. Eve was under no delusions, however. She knew that the blue skies with their puffy white clouds could all too quickly turn to dark rain clouds or even the heavy snow clouds that would change everything in the blink of an eye. She picked up her pace. Winter days were short enough here—she wanted to make sure she used every minute of the daylight she had to get the measurements she needed.

The climb itself was not too difficult, but Eve was glad she'd thought to bring the walking stick her father always carried. Recent rains had dislodged rocks and gullied the path, making it a difficult trek. After tripping and almost twisting her foot a second time, she reluctantly slowed her pace. Impatient as she was to get to the knoll, it would not do for her to suffer a serious injury or—God forbid—fall down the steep cliffs to the rocky beach below.

Rounding a bend in the path, Eve startled one of the ground squirrels that had burrowed a home in the cliffs. She stopped quickly and stepped back, but not before dislodging some of the rocks on the path ahead. A rockslide had eaten away part of the path, creating a dangerous gap. If she had not stopped for the small rodent, she could have easily fallen to her death. Sending a little prayer of thanks heavenward, Eve stepped gingerly off the path and worked her way through the brush and around the gap. The detour took longer than she'd hoped, and by the time she finally reached her destination, she had only a few hours left to work.

At the top of the knoll, she set up the bulky cross staff from which she could calculate altitudes and adjusted the quadrant to find the latitudes. The measurements garnered from these instruments were only the first step. After collecting the locations of as many points as she could, she'd do the triangulating calculations that gave her precise coordinates to plot on the huge map grid. The more points she could plot, the more accurate the final drawing of the map would be.

Obviously, it wasn't practical to map every curve on a coastline or every tributary that flowed into a creek. For one thing, these points could and did change with the tides and storms. Part of the job of mapmaking was to identify landmarks that were stationary and would stand for a long time. It was this part of the mapmaking process that was sometimes more art than science—an art that had been practiced for centuries. Even with all the modern instruments and scientific calculations, cartography was still very much dependent on the skill of the mapmaker.

This final map—her father's most important work—would provide the Crown with the most accurate picture of the British Isles that had ever existed. The intricate, detailed drawings would show the location of cities and towns in England, Scotland, and Wales as well as rivers, mountains, harbors, and beaches. It would also show many man-made landmarks, including roads, bridges, railroads, monuments, and castles. All of these were part of the story to be told by her father's map—a project that represented many years of Lord Tangier's life.

Lord Tangier was a scholarly man who had come into his title when his older brother died. By the time he received his letters patent, he had already made a name for himself as a brilliant mathematician and a talented illustrator. Upon finishing his studies at Cambridge, he had been asked to complete various commissions to create maps for some of England's smaller cities as well as some of its larger estates. Just a few years later, King George III asked him to do a new, comprehensive map of the British Isles. Her father had often wondered out loud if—after losing the war with the American colonies—King George simply wanted something to remind him of the kingdoms he *did* rule. Whatever the reason, Lord Tangier was more than happy to have the moniker, "Cartographer to the King."

After inheriting his title, Lord Tangier had been pressured to marry and provide an heir for the line, even though he had no interest in a wife. No one was more surprised than he when, nine months to the day after his one attempt to consummate his marriage, Eve was born. And no one was more delighted.

The sun had begun its descent by the time Eve had set up her instruments and started taking measurements. After only another hour, she packed up and made her way back to the cabin. That evening, as she sat by the fire working on some of the many calculations she needed to do, she couldn't help but think of the times when she and her father had done the very same thing—he doing the initial calculations and she checking his work. He almost never made errors, but he always double-checked every single calculation as a matter of practice. And, on that rare occasion when Eve did find a mistake, she and her father would celebrate her discovery with a silly toast: "To finding the compass needle in the haystack!"

Eve missed her father. He was a different man on their expeditions and on their rambles to this cabin—he was younger somehow. At least that's the way it seemed when she was with him on those trips. Perhaps it was the fresh air and exercise that gave him a more youthful presence. Or, perhaps it was the distance from her mother and the resulting freedom they both enjoyed in her absence.

Lady Tangier was a stickler for propriety and constantly concerned with what others thought of her and her family. Her obsession with London society and the consistently fickle *ton* was in sharp contrast to Eve's father, who spent as little time as possible out in society, despising the events that played out during the London season almost as much as his wife enjoyed them.

Eve could never understand how two such people, so completely opposite in every way, could be married to each other. The story her mother had told her about being seduced at her own wedding was understandable; the story that didn't make sense was how her mother and father were ever together in the first place.

Eve would have wagered a great deal that the seduction her mother said happened on her wedding night was not the only seduction that featured in her parents' marriage. A beautiful woman paying attention to a lonely, scholarly, wealthy, socially inept lord of the realm? It would not have been at all surprising to learn that her mother had used her own wiles to entrap Lord Tangier when she decided that it was time to find a wealthy, respectable husband—preferably one who was infatuated by her beauty and charm and might be less concerned about the state of her virtue.

Monsieur Jones had obviously done her mother a favor by helping to create a false narrative about her wedding night. Thank goodness the man had fled back to France. If he ever returned to England, he might start looking for people to leverage—people he could blackmail in return for hiding him from the authorities. Eve would not be surprised to find her mother's name at the top of that list. Wherever Jones was now, she was glad he no longer seemed interested in her mother.

Yawning, Eve decided to go to bed so she could get an early start in the morning. With any luck, tonight she would be too tired to dream.

Chapter 17

When Hill returned to Haversham House to deliver his report about Viscount Glenly to Whit, the first person he saw was Avery.

"Whit's been called to London," Avery told him. "He didn't say what it was about, but the call came last night, and the impression I got was that it came directly from Downing Street. He should be back tonight."

"Look at this," said Hill, pulling the folded papers from his coat and handing them to Avery. "These were in Glenly's saddle bag. He arrived at Glenhaven late last night—actually, early this morning—and locked this bag in his private study the minute he arrived. I was searching his study when he deposited the bag in the room, so I looked through it and found this. I don't know what those numbers or the drawing at the bottom mean—it looks like a map of some sort—but look at the names on the list."

"That bastard," growled Avery. "If I ever get my hands on Jones, I swear I'll…" Avery slapped the paper and looked up at Hill. "This proves what Whit was hearing. It's not enough for Jones to go after us, he's going after Vivian and Linney as well. I don't know about these other names, but Rose is obviously someone important to Edgewood. And Eve. My God, Hill, how does he know about Eve?"

"I don't know. I thought I had covered any tracks

that displayed my feelings for her, but obviously somebody told Jones that I was…that she was…"

In spite of the situation, Avery smiled at his friend's frustration. "Something you're trying to say there, mate? Go ahead. Spit it out. You were…what? She was…what? Is it possible that what you're trying to say is you're heels over head in love with her?"

"I don't suppose you gave her my message?"

"You mean the one where *I* tell your lady love that you're pining for her? I think that's a message you should have delivered yourself, don't you?"

"Past tense is probably correct. Between almost announcing my engagement to Nadine and my performance at your wedding, I've pretty much ruined any chance I had with Eve and destroyed any tender feelings she had for me—which, of course, was the point. I just wish I'd been a little less convincing. She'll never forgive me. Not in a million years."

Hill sighed, but then squared his shoulders and looked directly at Avery. "All of that is beside the point. Until we arrest Glenly, she's just going to have to get used to having me around."

"Arrest Glenly? Did you find enough to prove he's in league with Jones?"

"Not 'in league with' Jones. Avery, Glenly *is* Jones."

"Are you sure? Bloody hell!"

"After I found that list, I looked deeper into his bag. I thought it was just his clothes until I found a shirt wrapped around a dagger and then a cravat hiding a garotte."

"So it's always been Glenly? Jones was just an alias?"

"Yes. You know how we kept thinking we had seen him before? We had—but in a totally different context. It was years ago. Remember when you and I first went up to London? Do you remember the Secret Garden—you know the house run by Whit's friend Iris? We were, what? All of eighteen? And we thought it would be a lark to meet some of her flowers."

"I remember the Secret Garden, but I don't remember Glenly."

"He wasn't Glenly then—he hadn't inherited his father's title yet, so he was Bateman-Jones. Phillip Bateman-Jones."

"Bloody hell, Hill! You're right, it was Bateman-Jones. Jones! You remember he had that odd way of pronouncing some words? We never actually met him, but he was yelling and cursing so loud that everyone heard him."

"I remember Iris had him thrown out because he beat one of her girls so badly she later died. Iris told him if he ever came back, she would deal with him. We all assumed he was drunk. He was acting like a lunatic. Screaming at her and saying she couldn't throw him out and that he'd get revenge and show her. And saying that the police couldn't do a thing to him because he had friends in high places."

Avery shook his head slowly. "That's why Iris said, 'It won't be the police dealing with him if I ever see his face around here again.' I'll never forget the look in her eyes when she said that."

"We've got to make sure that Linney and Vivian and Eve don't leave here until we know what's going on and Glenly—Jones—has been captured."

"Hill, Eve's not here. I thought you knew."

"What?"

"She told Linney she couldn't stand to watch you flirting with all the other ladies or dance with you knowing that you didn't care for her. She left just after you did."

Hill was silent for a moment. His heart beat faster at the hopeful news that Eve still seemed to care for him, but it almost stopped when Avery told him she was no longer still safely at Haversham House. "Where did she go? Did she go home to Tanglewood?"

"I think she planned to stop there," said Avery, "but she told Linney she wanted to finish her father's map—you know, the one commissioned by the King—and to do that, she needed to go north to Blackwood Abbey, the Tangier estates at the northern border."

"Who went with her?"

"I don't know for certain, but I know she took her maid to Tanglewood, so I'm assuming she'll also take her to Blackwood. They had a footman traveling with them in addition to the coachman. Hill…"

"If anything happens to her, Avery, if…"

"Don't think about that. Just go. Find her. You're not going to feel right until you do. And when you do—can I give you some advice that my friend once gave me?"

"I've never been able to stop you before."

"Tell her you love her and don't let her go. And until this madman is dead or in the Tower, keep her with you. Don't let her out of your sight."

"That's big talk from a man who left his almost-fiancée in London without ever asking for her hand."

"We're not talking about me, we're talking about you—and by the way, in case you didn't notice? My situation worked out just fine."

"Does Lady Tangier know where Eve went?"

"You just missed her. Eve sent the carriage back for her mother and the woman finally left this morning. It's too bad—I'm sure Lady Tangier would have enjoyed having the Duke of Camberton riding with her." Avery smiled at Hill's grimace. "You know, if you marry Eve, Lady Tangier will be your mother-in-law. Perhaps she'll want to live with the two of you."

Hill turned to fully face his friend. "I know you think you're very clever and quite amusing, but—as your friend—it is my duty to tell you that you are neither of those things. Good day, your grace."

Avery's laughter followed him as far as the door. "Hill, stop. Come back—I was just teasing you. I've never seen you this earnest before. I'm not used to it. But listen, in all seriousness, there's something I do need to tell you. I already told Whit, but if you haven't talked to him yet, then you still don't know."

"Know what?"

"There's no gentle way to say this—"

"For God's sake, Avery, just say it!"

"Jones—I guess that means Glenly—is Eve's father."

"*What*? What are you talking about?"

"When Linney was at Terra Bella in that passageway outside Lady Tangier's room, Jones was in the room with the woman."

"Yes, I know that. That's why Linney didn't go in."

"Yes, but from the passage, Linney could hear their conversation. Lady Tangier said something about 'her Eve' and Jones interrupted her and said, 'you mean *our* Eve, don't you?' And Lady Tangier said, 'Yes, of course.

Our Eve.' When Eve came to tell Linney goodbye, Linney told her what she'd heard. Eve was stunned and of course went and confronted her mother. She left for Tanglewood right after that. I thought you should know in case you run into Jones somewhere. It might be important."

"It might be," agreed Hill. "I'm not quite sure why or how, but it could be."

"I'll catch Whit up when he returns. Is there anything else I should let him know?"

"I don't think so. Wait, the drawing on that list I gave you and the numbers at the bottom of the page. I can't figure out what the drawing shows and I don't know if the numbers are important or not. Give Whit the whole thing. Maybe he has people who can figure it out."

"I will and I'll tell him you've gone to find Eve."

Hill started back down the path to the stables from where he'd just come.

"Hey, Hill," Avery called out, "be careful. You and Eve. Be careful."

Hill turned and stopped, bowing slightly to acknowledge the words of his friend. "You too, your grace. And give my best to your wife." He smiled and then started back toward the stables. This time at a run.

****

There wasn't time to wait for Hensen. There wasn't any time to waste at all. Until he knew Eve was safe—preferably safe in his arms—he couldn't breathe properly, much less relax.

From what he'd gathered from his encounter with Glenly, the man was angry and definitely coming unhinged. He didn't know if the man had recognized him or not. Hopefully the little ruse he and Hensen had performed was confusing enough. With any luck, Glenly would not equate the drunken man in his library with the Duke of Camberton—the man who was supposed to be courting his sister.

Surely Nadine had mentioned Camberton's name when she asked her elder brother to attend the house party. But if Glenly was the one who had put Eve's name on the list, then he must have realized that the romance with Nadine was a charade. Was that the reason he'd arrived at his estate in the middle of the night? Was he there to confront Camberton? Had he also put two and two together and realized that it was Camberton who was in his library?

If Glenly *had* found him out, was he, even now, on his way to Tanglewood to find Eve—hoping to exact a more painful revenge on Camberton?

Hill had been instrumental in seeing Napoleon securely put away on Saint Helena. If Glenly knew of Hill's role in the emperor's imprisonment, he would have even more reason to take his revenge. But how had he found out about Hill and Eve? And could a man be so focused on revenge and retribution that he would harm his own daughter? The answers to these questions haunted Hill as he rode as fast as he dared in the fading light, but none were likely to find their way to Hill's spinning mind any time soon.

The sun set quickly, leaving a cold and dark winter night. Hill decided to stop at the next inn and change horses, and then continue on to Tanglewood. He had no doubt Glenly would ride through the night to reach *his* destination; he could do no less. He'd just have to be careful. The roads were good the whole way to

Tanglewood and, with any luck, the moon would provide light to travel by.

After a quick bowl of hot stew and a large pint of steaming grog, Hill was back in the saddle. His new mount was fast and sure-footed on the dark roads. The moon had yet to rise, but the stars were bright and provided enough light for riding. Hill quickly sighted the old familiar constellations and found comfort in the guidance of the polar star. A shooting star streamed across the sky and for a few minutes he was transported back to August and his time at Terra Bella when he finally acknowledged to himself just how much he'd fallen for Eve and how very much he loved her.

Chapter 18

To be honest, it had taken Hill some time to accept the whole idea of love and marriage. He had planned to spend his life traveling and adventuring around the world. Shaking his head at his own naïveté, Hill spoke encouragement to his horse who, understandably, questioned his risky pace on such a dark road.

In April of 1814, Hill had been part of the detail that escorted Napoleon to his first island prison off the coast of Tuscany. At the time, he couldn't help but be charmed by the Italian countryside there. The lush vineyards and olive groves that dotted the hills, but also the rugged coastline and the perfect beaches, spoke to him in a way he'd never experienced before. Suddenly his whole life had meaning, and he made plans to travel after he left the King's service—starting with the Tuscany Region of Italy. With Napoleon vanquished and banished, people were traveling across the continent again, and, thanks to his father, Hill and Henrianna both had learned several languages as children. At university he had also studied Greek and Latin, and he couldn't wait to put his education to good use.

But Hill's dream of traveling had been pushed aside by a series of unrelated events that happened over a period of only a few weeks: Napoleon escaped from Elba, Hill became the Duke of Camberton, and Lady Eve kneed him in the groin.

Smiling just a bit, Hill leaned forward to assure the mare that he knew what he was doing—not the case when he had approached the poorly disguised servant boy in the barnyard of the Dog and Pony Inn. A lad who, as it turned out, was Avery's friend, Lady Eve.

Hill shifted in his saddle as he recalled the intensity with which Eve had applied her newly acquired skill of discouraging men from bothering her. He'd nursed serious doubts about—among other things—ever being able to provide an heir for the title he'd only recently inherited and had kept his distance from Eve—at least for a while.

A very short while, he grinned, remembering.

****

Avery invited everyone to Terra Bella for an impromptu house party at the end of the summer, and while the Duke of Easton and his future duchess were busy planning their wedding and their future life together, Hill was falling in love.

He didn't mean to. He didn't really even want to. But there was something about Eve that made a newly minted duke—one who'd never seriously considered taking a wife—start thinking about rings and weddings and about making Eve his own for the rest of his life.

The first time he'd stolen a kiss from Eve, it was he who ended up being surprised. *His* kiss had quickly turned into *their* kiss as she slipped her arms around his neck and kissed him back with a fervor and an earnest innocence that aroused him like no woman had ever done before.

Kissing her was like finding a soft breeze on a hot summer day. The simmering heat behind her soft, soft lips was unexpected, and he immediately wanted more. Tasting her and feeling her quiver in his arms at his touch made him want to run his hands over every bit of soft skin to see how she responded. He wanted to feel the silkiness of her glorious red hair and twist it between his fingers as he slowly devoured her lips. They had been in a secluded but still public hallway, and he had backed her up against a convenient wall, stroking down her spine, cupping her bottom, and pressing his arousal against her as she molded her shape against his. When he finally broke the kiss, he was gasping for air. But when their eyes met, he knew he couldn't stop.

He had taken her lips again, owning them and then parting them to explore her mouth with his tongue. He had taken unimaginable liberties, but she had moaned her consent, baring her long neck to his lips and returning his kisses with a passion that rivaled his own. She met his tongue with the tip of hers, touching and tasting him, and he responded with desire, running his hands all over her as if staking his claim. He stroked the fullness of her breast, immediately awaking the semi-aroused tip that he circled and stroked with his thumb, plucking and fondling the sensitive flesh beneath her bodice.

He tried to put his need into words, but before he could, she moved in his arms, kissing him and nibbling on his bottom lip until he could stand it no more. A noise from the hallway offered him a spark of sanity, and he put his hands on her shoulders to pull her close to his chest, calming them both.

"Eve, we have to stop. If I go any further…well, I don't want to do something that we might both regret."

Eve froze and then looked up at him with hurt in her eyes. "I would never regret it," she whispered and then like a dandelion seed on the wind, she was gone.

The look in her eyes was like a blade through his heart. He *never* wanted to see her look like that again.

That evening after dinner, when Avery and Linney had sequestered themselves in the library, Hill sought her out. He found her strolling along the edge of the lake, trying to find a breeze off the cool water. "I think you misunderstood me earlier," he said walking up behind her.

She turned to consider him with her big gray eyes and then turned away. "You seemed rather clear about things. I was horribly embarrassed by my behavior. I consider you a friend, Hill, and I don't want anything to change that. Can you ever forgive me for behaving in such a wanton manner?"

"As I said, I think you misunderstood what I was trying to say. Will you please listen to me?"

With a deep sigh, Eve turned back to face him. "Truly, Hill. It won't happen again. I'm so—"

He put a finger on her lips to silence her and then moved it under her chin so that she had to look up at him. The moonlight shining on her hair turned it to the richest gold. "That will never do," he said. "In fact, I must insist that it happen over and over, again and again."

Her puzzled look made him laugh out loud. She narrowed her eyes and punched him on the shoulder. "You don't have to make fun of me. I'm already mortified."

"Ouch!" He caught her wrist before she could punch him again.

"Eve, what I'm trying to say is that I had to stop because I didn't want to stop. I knew that if I held you in my arms or kissed you for even another instant, I would go too far, too fast, and I would regret it for the rest of my life."

"You mean…"

He could hardly hear her whisper.

"I think I love you, Eve. I know I want you, but we can't just…you know…in the middle of a hallway."

"We can't?"

"Well, certainly we *could*, but we shouldn't. That's it. We shouldn't."

"Why shouldn't we?"

"Because…well, because…you're a lady."

"Yes, and you're a gentleman. It seems to me that those facts go on the plus side of the argument."

"I *am* a gentleman. And a gentleman does not ravage a lady in a hallway."

Eve giggled. "So, it's the *location* that's the problem?"

Hill raised an eyebrow and looked down at her. All of this was difficult enough without her poking fun at his dilemma.

"Exactly. Had we been in an orchard, say, or by the side of a road, then I could have just thrown you down in the dirt and had my wicked way with you."

Despite her bravado, Eve blushed a rosy pink at his words. "You could try," she retorted, turning her back to him and then glancing back over her shoulder. "I seem to recall that you were the one wallowing in the dirt at our first meeting, not me."

"Yes, but that was before you knew how it felt for me to kiss you, here." Hill dropped a kiss at the base of her neck just above her shoulder.

Eve shivered in spite of herself.

"And it was before you knew what it felt like for me

to touch you here." He stroked down her arm, smiling at the way she melted back into him. He leaned to whisper in her ear, "What I was trying to say earlier was that we had to stop because when I make love to you, I want to do it slowly." He kissed her shoulder. "Deliberately." He nibbled her ear lobe. "And I want to make you beg me for more."

"Really?" Darkness had settled in, but he could hear the smile on her lips.

"Yes, really."

She definitely did *something* to him—she made him think about things he'd never thought about before and made him feel in ways he'd never felt before. He wanted her more than he'd ever wanted any woman, and when he was with her it was so very easy to surrender to his desires and lose all control—like he had when they were exploring the castle ruins just a few days later. Luckily, he came to his senses and stopped before they went too far, but it was far enough that he felt obliged to immediately offer Eve his hand in marriage.

That's when they quarreled.

To say that Eve declined his offer was putting it mildly. After she threw his proposal back in his face, he had childishly stormed off and not spoken to her except when necessary for the rest of the week—not until the night before he left to return to London. In hindsight, he had to believe it was fate that brought Eve to him later that evening at the lake—both of them looking for a respite from the heat...and perhaps each other? Once they came together, the night was all about wooing, winning back his love and taking her to a place of pleasure as he made the case for why they should always be together.

That last night at Terra Bella, Eve's soft honeysuckle scent took on a magical quality of its own as he laid her down on the soft blanket he'd spread by the lake. They'd quarreled about the stupidest things, but everything had finally come round right and now he held her hand as he treated himself to kisses and caresses. She had the softest lips. He had truly never experienced anything as soft as those lips—softer than the downy feathers the birds used to line their nests. He wanted to lose himself in that softness and simply kiss her all night long—at least that was his plan until Eve took control of the kissing.

When she trailed fluttery kisses down his throat to his chest, Hill thought he would explode. She had no idea what she was doing to him and how she drove him to a point of losing all control. And still, she clung to his hand as if afraid he would vanish. Didn't she know that there was nothing in heaven or on earth that would tear him away from her?

Partly out of self-defense and partly because he wanted to make the night something she would always remember, Hill set his mind on bringing Eve pleasure instead of satisfying the throbbing desire she aroused in him. He knew that his clumsy efforts at the castle ruins had resulted in her first and only climax, but now he wanted to teach her slowly and thoroughly about the passion that was possible between a man and a woman and about all the things a man could do to please his lady love. Hill knew he had found the woman he wanted to spend the rest of his life with, and now he only needed to convince her.

The hollow sound of a bridge beneath his horse's hoofs brought Hill back from his reverie. He was just five miles from Tanglewood. And Eve.

Chapter 19

"The Duke of Camberton, your ladyship." Tanglewood's butler displayed only a slight hint of disapproval at receiving guests at such an early hour.

"What on earth is he doing calling on me now? What time is it?"

"It is half-past nine, milady. He is asking about Lady Eve. Shall I tell him that she is not here and has traveled to Blackwood Abbey?"

"Heavens, no," said Lady Tangier. "I'll receive the duke in the first parlor. Send Lacey up to help me dress. Wait! On second thought, I'll receive the duke here. Have Lacey bring up a tea tray."

It was an hour later before Yates finally announced the Duke of Camberton.

"Your grace! What a lovely surprise!" Lady Tangier curtsied as Hill entered the room. Her morning dress fit her trim figure perfectly and displayed a great expanse of bosom.

"Lady Tangier. Thank you for seeing me at such an early hour."

"Would you care for some tea, your grace? Or chocolate? I had both sent up, just in case. Some people never have anything but tea with their breakfast, but I find that a cup of chocolate is just the thing on cold winter mornings. Wasn't it a lovely wedding at Haversham House? I do think Easton and his little duchess will be very happy. Have you known her long? I remember that you and Easton grew up together."

"Yes, we did. Avery and I have been best friends since we were very young."

"Yes, my late husband, Lord Tangier, and I stopped at Terra Bella years and years ago. This was when Easton's mother was still alive. We had gotten lost in a blizzard. Eve was just a tiny thing."

"Yes, I was also at Terra Bella when you visited," said Hill, but Lady Tangier continued as if he had not spoken.

"I think Eve was in love with Avery even then."

For some reason, this both irritated and fascinated Hill, touching some long-forgotten memory. "I'm not sure what you mean by 'even then,' " he said.

"Oh, it's nothing—it's just that I always assumed that Avery and Eve would be married by now. That's what Easton's father had always wanted, you know. And, of course, Lord Tangier wanted nothing less than a duke for his darling daughter."

"To the contrary," said Hill, "I *don't* know anything of the sort. Eve and Avery have always been just friends." He smiled, remembering the little girl with the long red curls, and then came to his feet, interrupting Lady Tangier's ongoing monologue. "I beg your pardon, my lady. Might I speak to Eve now?"

"Eve? Why, no, your grace, you cannot."

"May I know why?"

"Well, you could, of course… I didn't mean that I wouldn't allow it. It's just that Eve is not here. She stopped here only so her maid could pack for their visit to Blackwood Abbey, the Tangier family estate in the north, at the Scottish border."

The news that Eve was not here jolted Hill.

"Are there enough staff to protect her at Blackwood Abbey?"

"Protect her? Protect her from what?"

Hill hesitated. The information about Glenly was secret. Only the top tier of Whit's network understood how all the pieces were fitting together. On the other hand, Lady Tangier was intimately familiar with the man they were trying to find and capture. And she, more than anyone else, understood how dangerous he could be.

"Protect her from a man known as Monsieur Jones. Perhaps you know the name?"

Lady Tangier went ashen at the mention of Jones. "Why would she need to be protected from him?"

"So you do know of him, then?"

"Yes…I, uh… He was an acquaintance of my late husband, but I hadn't thought of him in years. Why do you think he would be a danger to Eve? I'm sure he wouldn't do anything to hurt her."

"Are you willing to wager Eve's life on that?" Hill was angry now. The woman's half-truths and evasions could endanger Eve.

"I don't understand what you're talking about, your grace." Lady Tangier stood up and crossed the room to her dressing table.

"I'm fairly sure that you do, madam. Is it true that Jones is Eve's natural father?"

Lady Tangier gasped and turned to face him. "Who told you that?"

"That's not important. What *is* important is that we believe Jones is no longer sane. He is on a killing spree and is hunting down the men and women who helped put Napoleon on Saint Helena—specifically, he's out to kill the dukes who were instrumental in defeating Napoleon, and also their duchesses."

"Then what has that to do with Eve?" Lady Tangier's voice was shrill. "She's not married—and certainly she's not married to a duke. I tell you, she's in no danger from him. He would never hurt his own daughter."

"You and I both know better, don't we? Jones is deranged. Right now he sees Eve as associated with me. Was it you who told him of our connection? Perhaps when you saw him after you left Terra Bella this summer? *Someone* told him that I was in love with Eve. Was that someone you?"

"How could I tell him that? I told you, I haven't seen him in years. And I didn't know that you even cared for Eve. I don't…"

"Stop lying, madam. Eve is in danger. She's in danger because I'm in love with her and because somehow Jones knows that."

The panic in Lady Tangier's eyes was growing. "As I said before, Eve told me she was going up to Blackwood Abbey. She's bound and determined to finish that infernal map that her father…uh, that Lord Tangier was working on. She was rather upset when I saw her last, so there's a chance that she'll stay up there a while. Or she might go to the gamekeeper's cottage. Lord Tangier often took her there when he was working. It's a very secluded place near the coast but I don't know exactly where it is."

"And you've had no word from Eve?"

"No. She was angry with me when she left Haversham House, so I didn't expect to hear anything from her. But her maid sent word to my housekeeper that they had arrived in Blackberg."

"When was this?"

"I…I don't know. The housekeeper told me when I arrived here last night." Lady Tangier started weeping. "What if something happens to her? She is all I have left. Do you really think he would harm his own daughter?"

"I honestly don't know. The man is beyond reason, so I don't know what he's capable of or whether he will remember that Eve is his daughter. But even if he doesn't kill her, he could injure or kidnap her. Nothing is certain. How far away is Blackwood Abbey from here?"

"It takes us three full days in the carriage, but that's with all the servants and bags. You could get there faster on horseback, couldn't you? I'll have Yates pack you some food and have a fresh mount readied."

"Thank you. I'll send word as soon as I know something. In the meantime, you should also be on alert here. If Jones is looking for Eve, he'll come here just as I did and he'll be angry that she's not here. Have your servants tell him that Eve has gone back to London and that you are ill and not receiving. And then send word to the Duke of Whitley at his town home in London. Do *not* talk to Jones or try to intervene. He is unstable and extremely dangerous. Do you understand?"

"Yes, yes, I understand," sobbed Lady Tangier. "Just go, please. Please go and make sure that Eve is safe."

Chapter 20

Hill reluctantly slowed the black Arabian to a safer canter. He'd ridden for two days straight, stopping only to change horses, and it would serve absolutely no purpose to have the beast turn up lame just because the Duke of Camberton wanted to go faster through the darkness. The sun would rise in another few hours, as would the good folks of Blackberg, the small village that had grown up around Blackwood Abbey. Unlike the aristocracy, the farmers and bakers and innkeepers and servants were up at dawn. Lady Tangier didn't know whether Eve was staying at the main house or not, but the townsfolk would know. His first stop would be to the local pub—to break his fast, yes, but more importantly, to get information.

At the sign of the Three Crowns Inn, Hill left his horse to be watered and fed while he went in for what he was assured was the best breakfast in town.

"Welcome, my lord. Will you be having a meal with us this fine, cold morning?"

"I am much obliged," said Hill. "Bring it to the table, please. And tell me, has Lady Eve been through town? I have a message from her mother."

"Aye, she and that maid of hers arrived with that no-account footman just two days ago."

"So, she's up at the abbey, then?"

"Well, now, as I heard it, she's gone off to finish her

Papa's map. Out to the gamekeeper's cottage on the northern boundary."

"I assume she took the footman with her?"

"Didn't you hear me say he was no account? *He* says she wouldn't hear of it, but *I* say he didn't do a very good job of convincing her."

Hill was inclined to agree with the barkeep. "So she's out there by herself? How far away is this cottage? How long will it take me to get there?"

"Well, it's like I told the other gentleman, your grace. You can ride for a couple of miles, but then you'll have to go on foot. The cottage is perched up on a pretty good incline. Lots of rocks and boulders." The man looked Hill up and down. "You look to be in good health, so I guess it would take you just three hours on foot. After the hour's ride, of course."

"Of course," muttered Hill. Then he jerked his head up. "There was another man asking about Lady Eve?"

"That's right. Just yesterday morning. Fancy toff, but I didn't like the look of him nearly as well as you, so after I gave him the same information I just gave you, I started him off in the wrong direction—toward another one of his lordship's cottages." The barman grinned. "He'll be lucky if he ever finds his way back to civilization."

The man looked Hill squarely in the eye. "We take care of Lady Eve. Have ever since she was a tiny thing coming in here with Lord Tangier for lemonade. I've always been partial to redheads."

"I have the same problem," said Hill with a grin. "Thank you."

****

It was just like Eve to make things difficult down to the last step. The good thing was that if it was difficult for him to find Eve, then it would also be difficult for Jones—assuming it was Jones who had been looking for her. Hopefully whoever it was had been thrown off track and decided to seek other prey, or at least bide his time until Eve came out into the open again. With any luck, that gave Hill enough time to find her and make sure she was safe.

Hill dismounted and gave the reins of the horse to the stableboy to take back to the inn. He started down the trail to the cottage on foot. One thing was for certain. If he ever did find Eve, he was going to keep her right by his side—at least until Jones was captured. Or dead.

Hill briefly considered the fact that he and Eve would be alone together unchaperoned in the wilderness, but then he decided that it made no difference—she was going to marry him, so to hell with anyone who made noises about her reputation. Of course, the sooner they married the better, and if spending a few days with her alone in the woods condensed that timeline, then so be it. That was more than acceptable with him.

Hill had a niggling feeling in the back of his mind that perhaps Eve should be a part of this conversation, but he quieted the voice in his head with the rationalization that once she realized the situation, she would surely agree that a quick wedding was the only real path forward. She certainly *seemed* to want him—although that was several months ago and before their less than congenial encounter at Haversham House—but that was the agreement they'd made. Now was no time to second-guess that decision.

Using the directions given him by the proprietor of

the Three Crowns, Hill was making good time. Perhaps he should have asked if Eve had a weapon with her. He did not relish being shot at—and he certainly wouldn't put it past her.

As he had done many times on this trip, he wondered how Eve's name had made it onto Jones's—Glenly's—list. The only people who knew about how he felt about his summer spent with Eve were Avery, Linney, and Eve's mother—it had to have been Lady Tangier. Which meant she was still seeing Jones and had most likely told him about Hill's fascination with Eve. The lady was clear that she wanted a duke for a son-in-law, and, since Avery was no longer available, Hill's recent ascendance to the title would certainly be appealing.

Hill swore under his breath. Avery's words about the lady in question becoming his mother-in-law if he married Eve rang in his head. With a deep breath, he corrected his thinking: *when* he married Eve, not *if*. And, given enough money, perhaps Lady Tangier would enjoy an extended stay on the continent.

Chapter 21

The wind was picking up now, but it had been a most productive day.

Eve was glad she had gotten a lot accomplished because there was obviously a change in the weather coming. And from the looks of the clouds on the horizon, that change was coming sooner rather than later. Earlier in the day, she had hiked out to the little point that stuck out into the ocean, a piece of land that, on *her* map, would be named after her father—Lord Tangier. Just a small homage.

She had managed to get the measurements she needed, but had almost been stranded by the fast-moving high tide that rushed into the little cove beside the point and completely covered the narrow beach.

It was ironic that this stretch of coastline—belonging to the Tangier family—was so intricate. Like lace, it had scallops and detailed edges that, on most maps, would simply have been represented with a straight or perhaps a slightly curved line. Eve was taking great pleasure in gathering enough information to create a very detailed and extremely accurate rendering of the area. From her high point on the cliff above the changing sea, the visibility up and down the coast was amazing. She could see for miles, which meant not only could she take long-distance measurements, but she could also actually sketch the shoreline and compare those sketches with her calculated coordinates.

Not everyone would appreciate all the math that would happen before Eve finally started plotting the points for this final section on the map, but for Eve, spending the evenings in front of the fire with her journal of calculations was better than attending any party or soiree.

Humming to herself, Eve turned to see what inland landmarks she might be able to use. She could almost see Blackberg from here. Using her father's spyglass, she scanned to see if there were any trees or rock formations that stood out. Of course, there was her cottage off to the left and—

Someone was there!

With the spyglass, she could actually look into the cottage window and see a shadow moving about. Focusing the glass on the window at the front of the cabin, Eve saw the hook where she'd hung her hat yesterday. Someone had the audacity to hang *their* hat on the hook—as if they owned the place.

Had someone followed her here from the village? Certainly she'd made no secret about where she was going and had no reason to hide that she was staying at the cottage. Still, it was not an easy place to get to. No one just "happened by" and popped in for a visit. No, someone wanted to find her and had gone to a lot of effort to get here.

A man's back suddenly filled her view and with it a sneaking suspicion of who had invaded her privacy. When he finally turned around, Eve lowered the spyglass and shook her head. She couldn't believe her eyes!

What was the Duke of Camberton doing here?

Her beautiful, carefree, productive day was dashed

in an instant. A frisson of excitement was immediately replaced with concern. Was something wrong with Linney? With her mother? But as she watched the slow movements of the man in the cottage, it was clear that he was in no hurry to do anything. Besides, why would the Duke of Camberton take the trouble to bring her a message that a servant could bring?

With the shock of the moment wearing off, Eve's concern was replaced by a much larger dose of annoyance. Of *course* he would show up somewhere he wasn't supposed to be. However had he managed to tear himself away from all the ladies fawning over him? And why was he here? Alone? Didn't dukes always travel with an entourage?

Eve snapped the spyglass shut. "I cannot believe that he just showed up—uninvited! Every time I turn around, he's inserted himself into my life. What an arrogant, self-centered…arrogant…*man*!" The fact that no one heard her rant except the wind and perhaps a few seagulls mattered not.

"I'm sure he expects me to stop whatever I'm doing and attend to him. Well, his grace will be waiting a long time if he wishes to speak to me. For all he knows, I've gone somewhere else for tonight. There's more than one gamekeeper's cottage on my father's land." The fact that the other gamekeeper's cottages were miles away at the opposite edge of Tangier land only irritated Eve more.

"He doesn't get to control my life just by turning up whenever he pleases."

She turned her back on the view to the cottage and looked west to the sea, commanding herself to take a series of deep breaths. "I certainly hope his grace brought something to help him pass the time, because *I* will not be entertaining him. I'm not going to stop what I'm doing just because some duke has come here—uninvited—to annoy me. *He* may be able to live a life of leisure, but *I* have work to do."

Even in her agitated state, Eve knew she was being unfair. Hill worked harder than any man she'd ever met. Certainly he worked harder than all the other aristocrats she'd met at social events. Hill came into his title only a few years ago and was, as he'd told her at Terra Bella, still trying to catch up on all of his duties. It seems that the previous Duke of Camberton was not very concerned about the circumstances of his tenants. As a result, many of the farms on the lands Hill inherited were in great need of repair. In addition, there was still the farm where his mother lived and where he and Henrianna had grown up. His mother remarried after his father's death, but Hill's stepfather was interested only in the extra land that could be planted. He did nothing to support the rest of the estate—holdings that still belonged to Hill and Henrianna.

Grumpy with herself for defending the man who had broken into her house, Eve tried to refocus her thoughts on the task at hand. There were many more measurements she needed in order to map this coastline. She tripped over her bag and, for the hundredth time, cautioned herself to watch out for the crumbling ground at the edge of the cliff. If she lost her equipment over the edge, it would be nearly impossible to get it back. The only way down to that narrow beach was a steep set of uneven breaks in the cliffs, passing for steps. Not to mention that some of the more isolated beaches disappeared altogether at high tide, leaving only a direct drop into deep ocean.

After taking the same measurement for the third time, Eve sighed in frustration. Why couldn't she concentrate? Even before the thought formed in her head, she knew the answer.

It was all Hill's fault.

She felt like he was watching her—even though it was she who was watching him. She took out the spyglass and had another peek through the window of her cottage. His hat still hung on the hook. Knowing his grace, he had probably decided to fix himself something to eat with *her* food or take a nap in her bed.

Blast the man for ruining her day!

****

The little cottage hadn't been difficult to find—if you knew where it was. Tucked into the bushes at the edge of the forest, the tiny structure backed up to one of the stands of trees that made this area so different and so beautiful. Following the directions from the innkeeper had taken Hill on a footpath that paralleled the coastline and climbed as the terrain increased in elevation. He spotted the cottage at the edge of the woods about halfway up to the top of the point. It was a welcome sight for a man who'd had no sleep in three days.

Hill saw no sign of Eve as he approached the cottage—but then she was probably out doing…well, doing whatever it was she was here to do. He wasn't sure he understood exactly why she had decided to run off to the wilds of northern England and southern Scotland, but he would guess her mother was one of the reasons for her hurried flight.

And, if he was honest, he'd have to say that the other reason—possibly the *overarching* reason for her departure—was himself.

The one good thing about him finding Eve's name on Glenly's list was that he could now tell her about his mission and explain the danger she was in. In his mind's eye, he had envisioned the whole scene where he explained his secret assignment—including his recent dangerous encounter with Glenly—as Eve listened with rapt attention, shivering at his close encounter. In his imagination, he had Eve in his arms within ten minutes of telling her the story—eight minutes if he talked fast.

Between passionate kisses, she would apologize for her actions and for her tart words. Perhaps she would even shed a tear or two. He would "shush" her as he gently kissed her eyelids, her nose, and finally those lips. She might even cry with remorse at how she could ever have thought so ill of him when he had simply been doing his duty in service to king and country. He would, of course, graciously and nobly forgive her and soon everything would be back to the way it had been that last night at Terra Bella.

The only problem was that when he reached the cottage, Eve wasn't there.

Hill knocked on the cottage door and called her name, but there was no answer. He tried the door and found it unlocked, so, ducking to avoid hitting his head, he entered the tiny cottage and looked around. She had definitely been there—there were blankets and some clothes stowed neatly on shelves. The fire was banked, the bed had been slept in, and there was a wooden bread box in the middle of the table that contained a loaf of bread, some cheese, and two large pasties. There were also several books—journals, from the looks of them—in a stack on the table. For a place that hadn't been lived in for a while, it was quite tidy, and, even with the cold weather, it was cozy. But the place was empty and he had no idea where she was.

Three days of hard riding without sleep, to make sure she was safe, and the woman was nowhere to be found. How typical.

Hill hung his hat on the hook near the door and helped himself to bread and cheese while he looked around the cottage. Two windows let in daylight—one facing east and one west. He stood for a few minutes at the westward window, looking out over the ocean. He wished he had some idea of which way Eve had gone or how long she'd been away. The innkeeper seemed certain that his wily misdirection would be enough to confuse the other man looking for Eve, but Hill wasn't so sure. If it *was* Jones, it wouldn't take him long to figure out that he had been sent on a wild goose chase. The man was a brilliant spy, after all, with a vast array of skills and abilities. He would eventually find his way to this cottage and Eve if that was what he wanted.

Hill just hoped Jones didn't take out his anger on the innkeeper.

According to her maid, Nancy, Eve was continuing the map project her father had been working on when he died. Hill had seen the big map underway at Tanglewood. Evidently Eve was using her father's instruments to collect the measurements that would lead to coordinates being plotted on the large map. He saw no equipment in the cottage, which probably meant she had trudged off carrying everything with her and—

A flash of light caught his eye. It seemed to be coming from the top of the hill that ended abruptly at the steep coastal cliffs.

The light flickered again and Hill squinted to see if he could detect any motion at its point of origin. It seemed to be pointed at him—at least at the cottage—and seemed to be a reflection off something. A spyglass, perhaps? Surely a mapmaker had a spyglass as part of her equipment?

He smiled. Eve was watching him. He was sure of it. He quashed the desire to wave at her and instead stepped out of her view. It didn't look like she was that far away. He would give her time to come down and greet him, now that she knew he was here. It shouldn't take her more than an hour to get back to the cabin. And in the meantime, he'd take a quick nap. Three days was a long time without sleep.

****

When Hill woke up a few hours later, it took the plaintive calls of a seagull to remind him where he was. He frowned. Why wasn't Eve back? He stood to the side of the single window and looked out, noting that the sun was well on its way to the horizon. If that had been a reflection from her spyglass, she would have had plenty of time to return to the cottage by now.

He'd assumed the reflection was from Eve's equipment, but maybe he was wrong. It was time to find the lady, and the logical place to start was at the source of that light.

Leaving his hat, Hill slipped out of the cottage and circled around the back, deciding to approach his destination not from the path but from the woods on the other side. After a quick hike through the brush, he veered off the path and into the forest. He finally spotted Eve in a clearing at the edge of the cliff. His skills in the field on covert missions for Whit came in handy as he slowly approached her without making a sound.

When he saw her take out her spyglass, look toward the cottage, and then shake her head, he almost laughed. *What a stubborn thing she was!* He would wager any amount of money that she had decided not to go back to the cottage just because he was there. Her stubbornness was going to be the end of her, though. Where did she think she was going to spend the night? It was an unseasonably pleasant day with mild temperatures. But the wind was blowing and the minute the sun set, it would be January cold. Did she think to shiver outside while waiting for him to leave?

Hill rolled his eyes and moved in without a sound.

****

The knowledge that she was hidden from Hill's view from the cabin window relaxed Eve somewhat—although it did nothing to lower her level of pique. Hoping to calm herself, she started reviewing the measurements she'd taken that morning, comparing them to her master list so she could see what information she still needed.

Squatting to pull her journal from her pack, she turned to the pages where she had recorded her measurements. Remembering how her father would always let her write down the numbers when they were out together, she smiled to herself. "Two heads are better than one," he would say, "and four hands are better than two."

"You, madam, are a difficult lady to find."

Eve stood up with a start and instinctively took a step back. The ground beneath her feet crumbled and suddenly there was nothing.

As Hill watched in horror, Eve lost her balance. Screaming, she fell backwards down the rocky cliff.

Chapter 22

Ow!

Eve's first thought was to send up a thank-you that her father's equipment had not fallen with her.

Her second thought was that she had undoubtedly hit every rock on her way down and was going to be sore for days.

Her third thought was another thank-you that she was not dead and, amazingly, didn't seem to be seriously hurt.

Her fourth thought was for Hill, who had somehow managed to scramble down beside her.

"You!" She started to sit up, but cried out at a ripping pain in her shoulder. Hill pushed her gently back down to the ground and started running his hands all over her. In the back of her mind, Eve knew that Hill's extensive medical training—a product of his time leading men at the front early in Napoleon's war—was the reason for the groping and that the process was purely to feel for broken bones or any other injuries.

There was absolutely no reason for the other feelings that his touch stirred in her.

"Why are you here?" she said pushing at his hands with her good arm as they felt their way through her hair.

"Hush," said Hill, continuing his evaluation. He sat back on his heels. "You are without a doubt the luckiest person alive."

"Why? Because I survived your pushing me off the cliff?"

"I didn't push you. You stepped back and the ground crumbled beneath you."

"Because you *made* me step back."

"How did I do that?"

"You scared me. You crept up behind me and scared me and made me step off the edge of the cliff."

"The ground was already crumbling there! Which you would have seen if you'd taken the time to look around at your surroundings."

"So now you're going to lecture me about being careful? That's a laugh." Eve tried to illustrate her point with a guffaw, but ended up sucking in her breath at the pain that shot through her shoulder.

"Lady Genevieve, will you please shut it so I can see if there is anywhere else that you have caused yourself injury?"

Eve narrowed her eyes and glared at him but allowed him to finish his cursory examination.

"I don't think anything is broken—which I find truly hard to believe. I came close to breaking both my legs just making my way down here after you. You have lots of scratches and scrapes, and you're going to be one big bruise in the morning. I expect you'll have the mother of all headaches from bashing your head on those rocks, but other than your shoulder, you seem to be in relatively good shape. Now let's take a look at that arm. Here. Drink this."

A silver flask was thrust in her face. Instinctively she started to reach for it with her right hand, immediately grimacing at the pain. She awkwardly took the flask with her left hand.

"Do you need help?"

"I think I can manage to take a drink from a flask." Upending the flask, she took a long drink—and promptly choked, coughing violently. The coughing made her shoulder hurt and the tears that she had pushed away earlier returned with a vengeance.

"A sip might have been more prudent," Hill muttered. "I swear, you are your own worst enemy and the biggest danger to yourself. I should lock you up in a tower and throw away the key."

"I assumed it was water, not spirits."

"Do you hurt anywhere else?" he asked.

Eve shook her head as she bit her bottom lip trying not to cry. The more appropriate question would be was there anywhere that she *didn't* hurt.

Gently, Hill helped her sit up, positioning her right arm so that it was cradled against her chest and effectively immobilizing her shoulder. He stood up and removed his coat. Then he took off his weskit and put his coat back on.

"What are you doing?"

"I'm going to wrap this around you to keep your arm from moving."

Carefully he threaded her good arm through one of the armholes of his vest and wrapped the rest of the garment around her injured arm and shoulder. He buttoned the front snugly over her own coat.

"Can you stand up if I help you?"

Eve nodded her head, hoping it was true.

Hill moved behind her and helped her up by the waist, standing her up as if she were a doll.

"Let's get away from the edge of the water. It looks like the tide is coming in, and we don't want to get any wetter than we already are."

Supporting her by keeping one hand on her good arm, he guided her around the boulders and back toward the cliffs, helping her sit down on a big rock with a slightly flattened top.

"Stay here and I'll go find the way back up."

"That's going to be a problem."

"What? Why?"

"Because this is one of the beaches in the area that's totally cut off, except at very low tide—which, as you remarked, has already happened. And even then, you sometimes have to wade through water to get over to the other beach. What I can't remember is whether or not this is one of the beaches that vanishes completely at high tide. Can you tell? It looks like that's the high-water mark on the cliff behind us."

"By 'vanishes completely at high tide,' you mean 'is completely submerged at high tide'?"

"Right. The locals usually post signs on the headlands for those beaches, and I don't remember seeing any, so I think we may be fine."

"You *think*?"

"We'll have to wait until low tide again and then we'll be able to get to the next beach and find a way up. Low tide was a little after noon, so it won't be low again until after midnight."

Hill sighed as he stood up. "And I thought Monsieur Jones was our biggest problem."

"Wait, what? Is he back in England? Where are you going?"

"That, my love, is a long story. And one which I expect I will have more than enough time to relate to you. Right now, I'm going to see if I can find a better place for us to escape the high tide and wait for low tide before it gets completely dark."

"I'll go with you," said Eve. She struggled to stand up with her injured limb but lost her balance and sat down again. "I *can* walk, you know," she called after Hill.

Hill either did not hear her or chose not to acknowledge that he heard her as he walked down the narrow strand of sand and rocks.

Chapter 23

"That didn't take long," said Eve, glad that Hill had returned so quickly. In the few minutes he was gone, the sun had slipped below the horizon and the wind had grown stronger. She was shivering, which made her shoulder ache even more.

"I found an indention in the cliffs—a kind of shallow cave. I couldn't see how far back it went, but we should be able to go in far enough to get out of the wind and stay dry at high tide. I could see the high water mark on the beach in front of the opening."

He frowned when he saw Eve shivering. "You should have worn a heavier coat."

"You're right. What was I thinking? I should have dressed for the possibility of being pushed over a cliff and spending the night underwater on a windy beach."

Hill put one arm around her and helped her stand. He kept his arm in place, helping her navigate the rocky beach in the dying twilight. "I didn't push you," he growled. "Would you please stop saying that?"

"Fine. I was standing at the top of a cliff. You appeared and I fell to the bottom of said cliff. Is that better?"

"Actually I would prefer that you leave me out of it entirely. You fell when the ground crumbled beneath your feet because you were standing too close to the edge. The cave is just a little bit farther."

"Yes or no? Would I have fallen if you hadn't suddenly appeared up there on the top of the cliffs?"

"How can I answer that? I don't know how long it would have taken the ground to crumble or what kind of balance you have. You might have tripped over your tripod, fallen on your head, and killed yourself with me nowhere in sight. Or you could have been looking through that spyglass of yours and stepped off the edge all on your own."

"How do you know I have a spyglass?"

"I saw it reflecting the light when you were up on the cliff spying on me. That's how I knew where you were."

"So it *was* you in my cottage. I could have shot you, you know."

"I suppose that's possible in theory, but not very likely in practice. Do you even *have* a firearm with you?"

Eve didn't answer.

"No," said Hill. "I didn't think so. You probably have never even *held* a gun, much less fired one."

"I'll have you know that I always participated in my father's shooting parties."

"Is that so? Were you simply loading the clay pigeons or did you actually handle the guns?"

Eve's silence confirmed that he had scored another direct hit. She quickly changed the subject.

"You never answered my question. Why are you here? And how did you find me? The last time I saw you, you were feeding Miss Banbury a piece of Linney and Avery's wedding cake and whispering in her ear. Were you perhaps instructing her on how to eat? Was she unable to feed herself?"

Hill smiled. So she'd noticed that, had she? She

must have been watching him rather carefully. Miss Banbury was one of Whit's operatives and, at that particular moment, they were actually working, trading information that Miss B. had gleaned from one of the servants.

"That's more than one question, but here's the answer. I came to find you and I simply followed the trail you left."

"You went to Blackberg?"

"Yes, and I talked to Nancy and to her mother and to the innkeeper in town who thinks I'm up to no good. And before that, I went to Tanglewood."

"Tanglewood? You spoke to my mother?"

"I did indeed."

"You must have been *very* desperate to find me."

"I told you I was."

In addition to a dry spot out of the wind, the cave also offered a relatively smooth wall to lean against. Hill helped Eve to the side of the cave and settled her against the wall. He sat down on her left side and pulled out his flask again.

"Here. Take another sip from this. That's it. Now just lean against me and try to get some rest. We have nothing to do until midnight, and you'll need your strength." He gently put his arm around her and pulled her close.

Exhausted, in pain, and grateful for something soft in a cave of rocks, Eve slowly relaxed against his warmth and closed her eyes. The fresh scent of balsam and the comforting beat of his heart lulled her until, finally, she slept.

****

"Has the tide gone out yet?"

Eve tried to sit up. At some point in her slumber she had gone completely horizontal. Her head was pillowed by half of Hill's huge coat. The other half had been draped over her prone body as a blanket. At the rate he was giving her his clothes, he would be naked before midnight. She smiled to herself and had to stifle a slightly hysterical giggle which reminded her of her injured shoulder.

Hill stood up from the fire he had managed to build at the entrance and raised an eyebrow at her laughter. The warmth from the fire penetrated into the damp cave, and while she was still chilly, it was certainly not as cold as it could have been.

"The tide has definitely turned," said Hill helping her into a sitting position. "But it still has a ways to go before we can make our escape. I think I saw a set of steps carved into the cliff down the beach, although 'steps' may be a bit of an exaggeration. But it did look like there was a path of sorts. How do you feel?"

"Better. My shoulder hurts, but it's not as bad as it was."

"Sleep is often the best thing to do for an injury," said Hill.

"Where did you learn how to do what you did?"

"What? Build a fire?"

"No. How did you learn to check for injuries on someone who's been hurt?"

Hill shrugged. "It's not that much. I just tried to stabilize your shoulder to keep you from injuring it more by moving it. My mother knows a lot about healing, and when she was teaching my sister, I tended to listen in. Most of it is just common sense. At the front in France,

I spent some time at the hospital helping the doctors and nurses. You learn a lot just by watching others. I've never had any formal training, if that's your question—although, before I inherited the title, I was thinking about going to Italy to study medicine."

"You didn't want to go back to your family's farm?"

"I wouldn't have minded doing that, but my mother remarried and my stepfather is an arse. That's the nicest thing I can say about him. To be fair, I'm pretty sure he feels the same way about me. So, no. That wasn't an option with him there."

"Is your sister still there?

"She's in Paris, remember?"

"That's right. What is she doing now that Napoleon has been defeated?"

"I don't know and I really don't want to talk about it."

"She's your only sibling, right?"

"Yes. Is this your idea of not talking about it? Because I have to tell you, you're not doing a very good job of it."

"Fine. Although if I had a brother or sister that I didn't know where they were, I'd be worried. Are you worried?"

"Of course, I'm worried about her, but right now I'm worried about you. So can we not talk about Henrianna?"

"Let me guess: your father's name was Henry and your mother's name was Anna. Am I right?"

"Eve!"

"Just tell me whether I'm right or not. She was named after your parents, right?"

"No. As a matter of fact, you're wrong. I was named after my father and Hen was named after my mother's parents—our grandparents, who hated the fact that their daughter had married a man with no money and no title. It was an effort to appease them, but it didn't work. They never came to visit and they never talked to my parents. When my father died, they didn't even send a letter of condolence to my mother. If they had, if they had shown some compassion or some support, then maybe my mother wouldn't have had to marry our neighbor. But they did and she did and Henrianna ran off with some titled gentleman and then ended up being the mistress to one of Napoleon's generals. Does that answer all of your questions? Now can we talk about something else?"

"Your grandparents must be kicking themselves a bit now that you're Camberton. They do know, don't they?"

With a laugh, Hill sat down beside Eve. "Do you never stop?"

Eve bit her bottom lip and was finally quiet.

"Well, don't stop now," said Hill. "We have a lot of time to kill. What other questions do you have? And just to answer that last one, I honestly don't know whether my grandparents know that their grandson—the son of the man they ignored and put down for years—is a duke of the realm. I guess I hope they do, but if I'm totally honest, I really don't care. What's next?"

"You never did answer my question about why you are here."

"I told you I came to find you."

"But why?"

"Because you weren't at Tanglewood."

"That's not an answer and you know it. Why were you trying to find me? When I saw you at the wedding, it was clear that you had no interest in me. Why did you all of a sudden need to find me? Why the change of heart?"

"There was never a change of heart—"

"Hill! When we were at Terra Bella, you…you said you loved me. We kissed and…well, you know."

"Yes," said Hill in a low voice, "I *do* know."

"And then that night at the lake, we… You said you would write to me, but I never got a letter or heard anything from you. You asked me to marry you, for goodness' sake. I know we agreed that you would take back your offer, but you did ask me…and then you just disappeared."

"That was a mistake," said Hill bluntly.

Eve's heart stopped. How could she have been such a fool? It *was* all a lie. Eve shook her head as if to clear it of those lingering thoughts. Obviously she had misread…everything. Obviously when he had told her how beautiful she was, it was the same line he'd spoken to scores of other girls. Obviously he meant more to her than she did to him. He truly was simply enjoying a summer romance. Nothing significant. The same way he had done—what—scores of times before? She was just another in a very long string of dalliances. How *could* she have fallen so completely, so totally in love with someone who didn't feel the same about her?

She turned away from Hill.

"It was a mistake," he repeated, "not to insist that you marry me right then and there. If we had been engaged, if you had been my fiancée, then I would have had a better case to make to Whit and perhaps I could have told you then about the secret mission he sent me on."

"*What?* What are you talking about?"

"If you and I had been engaged, I could have persuaded Whit to let me tell you why I was gone and what I was doing. He believed it would be better to get your honest reaction to my jilting you, but knowing you, I feel certain that you could have played the part quite well."

Eve shook her head. The headache Hill had foretold had made its appearance with a vengeance. "I don't understand. A secret mission? Whose mission? What secret? I don't understand."

"Perhaps let me explain, and then you can ask as many questions as you want."

Eve nodded her agreement.

"While I was at Terra Bella this summer," started Hill, "I got a message from the Duke of Whitley to return to London. Whit is…" Hill hesitated. How much was he at liberty to divulge to her? This particular secret was not his to tell.

"Whit is a spy. Yes, I know that," said Eve. "Linney told me a long time ago. Vivian explained it all after Monsieur Jones kidnapped her. When Whit and Avery and Lord Edgewood foiled the kidnapping and rescued Vivian, Jones decided to take out his anger by getting back at Whit. That and because Whit is in charge of all the king's spies, right?"

So much for secrecy, thought Hill. He wondered if Whit knew that Vivian knew so much about his activities. He wondered if Avery knew everything that Linney knew.

"Ah…well, yes. That is correct. And you remember that Monsieur Jones is an extremely dangerous man?"

"Yes, you told me that when we were hiding from him at Terra Bella."

"Very well, then. Did I also tell you that he is most likely insane?"

"You said he was dangerous. I didn't know he was mad."

"That's a relatively recent development, but it's a factor in why I came to find you. When Whit sent for me this summer, the mission he gave me was to find out Jones' real identity. We knew he was a member of the British aristocracy, and there had been rumors that he was somehow connected to the current Viscount Glenly. The Glenly family is a very old line, very respected and—at one time—very wealthy. They have always been extremely loyal to the monarchy—the current viscount's father was a great personal friend of King George. So, when we first came up with the idea that the current Lord Glenly is a traitor—well, we had to be sure. We had to be certain and we needed evidence. We couldn't just make accusations without having incontrovertible proof."

Hill leaned back against the cave wall. "The mission Whit sent me on was for me to pretend to court Glenly's younger sister, Nadine. To make it look as real as possible, I first had to make it look like I had cut things off with you. Too many people had seen us together and might have thought that you and I…"

Hill reached out to tuck an errant strand of hair behind her ear, letting his finger trace the outline of her face. "Well, anyway, I needed it to look like I was playing the field again. Only then could I pretend to fall for Nadine and be invited to family gatherings where I could look for evidence that tied Glenly to Jones."

"Why didn't you just tell me this?"

"Because it was a *secret* mission. For the King's

spymaster. Only a few people knew about it. What was I supposed to do? Send you a letter with all the details?"

"You could have come and told me in person. I would have kept your secret."

"I wanted to, but Whit said no. It wasn't you—it was your mother we didn't trust. She told you that she had not been in contact with Jones for years, and yet we know she saw him at Terra Bella this summer and we suspect she's seen him many other times as well. Whit thought it would be safer for you if you didn't know about my mission."

"So, your story was that you had jilted me and had started keeping company with Lord Glenly's sister, is that right?"

"Well, there were a couple of ladies before her. I wanted to make it look real—not like I was targeting her."

Eve rolled her eyes. "Honestly, you think every woman wants you, don't you?"

"I never said that. In fact, I doubt seriously if it is true."

"Of course it's true. Do you *see* the way women look at you? They are all trying to seduce you. The old ones and even the young ones who don't even know what seduction is."

"I hardly think that can be considered my fault."

"Of course it's your fault. You're perfect. You have soft, thick hair and those eyes that seem to be able to see into your soul. You treat women like they are goddesses and make each one feel like she is the only one you care about—that you only exist for her. No other man even comes close."

"Eve, you're arguing in circles, darling. Are you

angry at me because of what women think about me?"

Eve scowled at him. "I'm not your darling. Don't you dare condescend to me."

"I'm just trying to understand why you are so angry at me. You're comparing me with other men and finding them lacking?"

"I'm doing nothing of the sort. I'm merely cataloguing all your…your…your…all the ways you so obnoxiously allure women. And then there's the part about how you listen to them."

"Let me make sure I understand what you're saying. You're angry because I'm courteous and respectful and often interested in what women are saying?"

"Yes! No!"

"And you're comparing me with other men and I'm excelling?"

"You are without a doubt the most arrogant, egotistical, conceited man I've ever met. I don't know why I allow you to torment me."

"Is it perhaps because you are jealous of my relationships with other women?"

"Why in heaven's name would I be jealous of you? Of them? Please continue with your story. After you worked your way through the ladies of the *ton,* then what?"

"And then I was introduced to Nadine at a ball where I danced three dances with her."

"You did not! Three dances? Three? You might as well have put an announcement in the *London Mail*."

"Just so you know, my love, none were waltzes."

Eve glared at him. "I suppose it was all over the gossip columns the next day."

"Yes, it was. Which was exactly what we wanted.

After that, I went to all the same social events to which she was invited. I took her driving and walking in Hyde Park, and we went for ices at Gunters."

"Did you kiss her?"

"You mean other than a very proper kissing of her hand?"

"You know what I mean. Did you *kiss* her?"

"As a matter of fact I did not. I was a perfect gentleman."

Eve raised an eyebrow.

"It's true!" Hill shrugged his shoulders. "Actually it really is. I'm not saying that I *wouldn't* have kissed her if the situation required it. I was undercover, remember. I was trying to make things look as real as possible. But I wanted to save something in case I got in trouble at some point. You know, as a distraction." He hesitated. "The thing is…"

"What? The thing is what? I beg of you, your grace, don't stop now."

"The thing is that Nadine is no lady. That's what. I spent most of our time together trying to keep *her* from kissing *me*. She kept trying to put us in all sorts of compromising positions. Every time I saw her, she would pull me into a closet or behind a bush or down a deserted walk where she would try to steal a kiss or rub herself up against me. She would move my hands to inappropriate places on her person, and the gowns she wore… They were all so low cut that I was afraid her breasts would fall out if she leaned over too far—and she did like to lean over. A lot. She was constantly surrounded by gentlemen watching her lean over." Hill paused for a moment, remembering.

For her part, Eve was trying very hard not to laugh.

It was not only humorous but educational watching Hill be on the other side of this issue for once—taking the role of the fox rather than the hound. She couldn't help teasing him. "Your grace! Are you saying that Nadine leaned over *on purpose* just to get the gentlemen's attention?"

Eve pretended to be shocked, but had trouble keeping a straight face. He was so serious about Nadine using the oldest trick in any young lady's playbook. His next observation took the smile off her face.

"In her defense, she *did* have very nice breasts—as any man in London can attest."

"So, like all the other gentlemen, you spent a lot of time admiring and assessing her breasts?"

Hill saw the warning signs but for some reason chose to ignore them. "I did. Although, ironically, as I was playing the role of potential suitor, I had to appear displeased that others were ogling her. But honestly, I couldn't really blame them. They were extremely nice breasts to ogle."

In the silence that followed, Hill could hear the lapping of the sea on the vanishing beach. He tried to make amends. "You do realize that everything I did was done for king and country?"

Eve laughed in spite of herself. "Really? That's the best excuse you can come up with? That you ogled Nadine's breasts for king and country?"

"It was not easy to put her off, and I didn't want to make her angry. She is a very insistent and very persistent young lady—and I use that term loosely. No lady *I* know acts that way."

"So, you're saying that if a woman was to be a little aggressive about what she wanted, that you would consider her unladylike?"

"Exactly."

"So, for example, if a woman kissed you first, you would consider her to be unladylike?"

Warning bells were again ringing in his head, but Hill was on the path of pursuing righteousness. He wanted—no, he *needed*—to explain.

"A gentleman likes to be the one to initiate romantic overtures with a lady. She, of course, is then free to allow or rebuff his advances. But if a *lady* initiates a romantic interaction, then, as a gentleman, I am required to welcome her advances. It would be ungentlemanly of me to reject her."

"Obviously I have not completely understood this whole gentlemanly code of conduct thing," said Eve. "Let me see if I have this right. Any woman who is bold enough to say what she wants is practically guaranteed acceptance and can then take any liberties she wants to take as long as the man is living his life according to the generally established rules of gentlemanly conduct. Is that correct?"

"Well, I'm not sure that 'any' liberty is quite correct. I am certain there are *some* things that even a gentleman would not agree to—although I'm unable to think of one at the moment. But, for example, if in the late summer, a lady found herself on a blanket with a gentleman beside a lake in the middle of the night and decided she was in the mood for kissing, she's pretty much guaranteed to be successful."

Eve furrowed her brow. Exactly when had the tables been turned on her? Just seconds ago she was making fun of him and now he was saying that the only reason he returned her kisses when they were at Terra Bella was because of the requirements associated with gentlemanly manners?

Hill leaned over and put a kiss on the back of her neck. "Two can play this game, can they not, madam?"

Eve sputtered as she tried to formulate a response.

"No," said Hill. "Don't even try. Just acknowledge that I'm not as naïve as you seem to think I am. You and all your lady friends think you know all about manipulating your men. I think you should consider the possibility that your men enjoy being manipulated every now and again."

Eve smiled. He was indeed a worthy opponent.

"And just for the record," he said, his voice husky with desire, "*any* time you would like to take the initiative in a romantic overture, I will be more than happy to support your efforts in any way I'm able."

And that's when Eve decided that in spite of her arm being in a makeshift sling and still throbbing, and in spite of the fact that they were both dirty, sandy, and wet as they waited for low tide in that shallow cave on that narrow strip of beach, that in spite of all that, she wanted to initiate a romantic overture in the very worst way.

****

"Did you ever tell her that you loved her?" Eve was lying in Hill's arms. After a rather intense period of kissing, they had both dozed—at least she hoped he had too. It was odd, she thought, to be in such a perilous situation with the tide and at the same time to feel so utterly safe…and loved.

"Eve…that's not fair. I told you I was on a mission."

"I know. It's understandable if you did. I just wanted to know."

Hill was deliciously close to her ear when he whispered his response. "I have never said 'I love you' to anyone but you. Now go back to sleep."

****

Only a few hours more and they would be able to make their way across to an adjacent beach with access up to the cliffs. Hill stood up to stretch as Eve clumsily adjusted her own position.

"How did you finally get invited to Glenhaven?"

"We knew that the family—including Glenly himself—always gathered at Glenhaven after the holidays. I told Nadine that I wanted to speak to her brother about something very special, letting her think I was planning to ask for her hand in marriage. Right before Christmas, she sent me an invitation to come to Glenhaven after New Year's Day, but then she sent me a message that Glenly would be arriving at Glenhaven sooner than she'd expected. That's why I left Haversham House right after the wedding breakfast—so I could get to Glenhaven and start my search before the viscount arrived."

"You left before the ball? I did too. I…uh…I had to get home to Tanglewood."

"Avery seemed to think that you left so you wouldn't have to spend any more time around me. Was he mistaken?"

Eve blushed and looked away as she remembered telling Linney how she couldn't bear to watch Hill flirt with all the beautiful ladies when she still loved him.

"No, not exactly. I did say that, but then—" Eve stopped. She'd forgotten all about the rest of the conversation she'd had with Linney. The conversation where she had learned that Monsieur Jones was her father. Her heart sank. What would Hill do if he found out? There was no way he would want to be associated with the daughter of Napoleon's spymaster—the man whose identity he sought to uncover. The very reason for his mission. Eve felt ill.

"Are you in pain, my love? Is it your shoulder?"

If he knew, thought Eve. She couldn't imagine the disgust he would feel that he'd even been involved with her. That he'd kissed her. That he had almost married her. Her heart ached. She would have to tell him. He had to know.

"I…I'm fine. Just a twinge from my shoulder when I moved. Continue your story. What happened when you arrived at Glenhaven?"

"Glenly showed up in the middle of the night and I almost got caught."

Hill felt rather than heard Eve catch her breath. "But in the end, I found the evidence Whit wanted. I found proof not only that Glenly and Jones are connected, but that Glenly *is* Jones. I found the weapons Jones used to kill so many of our people, hidden amongst Lord Glenly's clothes. But I also found some papers—that's the real reason I'm here. On one paper was a list of all of us who have been on special missions to help find Jones. Whit, Edgewood, Avery, and I were at the top of the list. That was expected. We knew Jones was trying to eliminate Whit and his lieutenants. What was new was on the other paper. It had a rough sketch and some numbers at the bottom, but at the top of the list were our names again followed by the names of women. Beside Whit's name was written 'the codemaker' and beside Avery's name was written 'Linea Braddock.' Beside

Edgewood's name was written 'Rose du Bois' and some other names I didn't recognize, and beside my name was the name of a lady I had pretended to court before Nadine. But her name had been marked out and replaced by your name, Eve. Jones is seeking retribution not just by threatening us, but by threatening the women we love."

Had she heard correctly? *The women we love?* And that included her? Hill was talking again. She needed to pay attention.

"Whit had been called to London, so I gave the papers to Avery and told him to tell Whit what I found. And then I came to find you."

"Did Avery know what the drawing was or what the numbers meant?"

"No. At least he didn't when I showed them to him. I think he was going to take them to Vivian and see what she could make of them, but I didn't wait to hear otherwise."

Hill turned to face Eve and took her left hand in his. "That's why I'm here, Eve. *That's* why I've ridden for three days without sleep, suffered through an audience with your mother, hiked miles to a cottage at the edge of the wood, and thrown myself down a cliff. I was frantic that Jones would get to you before I could, that he would find you before I had the chance to tell you what he already knew. What I already knew. I love you, Eve. I've loved you since you kicked me senseless in the barnyard. I've wanted to tell you so many times, but I didn't want to upstage Avery and Linney. And then I didn't want to say anything until I'd finished my mission for Whit. But I don't want to wait anymore. I want you, Lady Genevieve, and I want everyone to know how very, very much I love you."

Eve could not keep the tears from falling. She clung to his hand as he continued.

"I think I've loved you since that first time I met you when you were only three."

Hill brought her dirty, cut fingers to his lips and kissed them gently. "And, if you will forgive my sense of timing and my choice of place, I want to ask you to marry me. Again. But this time I want to do it right and for the right reasons. You already have my heart, Eve, will you also accept my hand? Will you? Will you argue with me for the rest of my life and try to reform my worthless self? Will you forgive me for all my many faults and love me in spite of them? Will you allow me to love and cherish and protect you? Will you let me go to sleep every night holding you in my arms and let me open my eyes every morning to look into your eyes only? Will you love me to distraction and let me make love to you until we are both exhausted? Will you take me to have and to hold in sickness and in health and make me the very happiest of men? Will you marry me and be my only true love forever?"

The crisp, cold night was silent while it waited breathlessly for her response.

"Please, Eve. Tell me you love me. Tell me that you will be mine forever."

Eve raised the hand holding hers to stroke her cheek and then kissed the backs of his fingers. The man she loved and adored and desired with every part of her being was asking her to be his wife, his lover, and his friend forever. It was everything she'd dreamed of since she'd fallen in love with him. And yet…

How could she say yes, knowing who her real father

was? She couldn't subject Hill to such shame. She couldn't agree to marry him when her natural father—the man whose blood ran in her veins—was responsible for the deaths of so many British soldiers. A traitor who, even now, was plotting to kill this man and his friends.

Eve searched for the right words. Hill was looking at her for an answer. She could feel the tension rising as he waited for her response.

"Eve, will you? Will you marry me?"

Quick—before she changed her mind. She had to tell him the truth about Jones.

"Yes."

Chapter 24

Hill couldn't remember the last time he'd felt so happy. What did it say about his life, he wondered, that he felt the happiest and most relaxed that he'd felt in years here in the cold, dirty, damp sand and in very real danger of drowning? He smiled to himself. He'd left out the most important part of the equation: Eve was in his arms.

"Eve?"

Hill whispered her name and stroked the hair off her forehead. They'd both dozed off again as they waited for high tide to recede. He gently shook the sleeping woman beside him. "Eve, it's time to go. Wake up, my love. The tide is low enough for us to get to the other beach."

Eve sat up with a start. "What?"

"We need to go," said Hill. He stood up and offered his hand to Eve. She took his hand and pulled herself up.

"How can you tell that the tide is at its lowest?"

"I can't see the water any more. When we came in last night, we could see the waves—even though they were rather far down on the beach. I expect even at low tide we're going to get our feet wet, but I don't know how much time we have, so we should go. How do you feel?"

"Not as bad as I look, I'm sure, but I'm afraid to unwrap my shoulder until we're out of here."

"I agree. Just wait. We'll have the doctor look at it

once we're back in town. Right now we need to focus on getting back to the cottage."

The narrow stretch of sand that connected to the other beach was surprisingly dry when Hill and Eve walked across, and the steps Hill had found in the cliff proved to be steep but quite navigable. After resting just once along the way, Eve and Hill found their way back to where they'd started. The waning gibbous moon proved a godsend, shining enough light so they could see that Eve's things—her father's precious tools and Eve's pack and journal—were still there.

Under Eve's watchful eye, Hill carefully packed up the instruments and carried them back to the gamekeeper's cottage. Settling Eve on a pallet before the hearth, he stirred up the fire, adding two logs to take the chill off the small room.

"There's still another hour or two before dawn," he said, sitting down beside her in front of the fire. "Why don't you try to get some more sleep."

"I couldn't possibly sleep," replied Eve. "There's too much going on in my head."

"Care to share some of those thoughts?"

"The biggest one is actually more of a question."

"Tell me. Maybe I can help with an answer."

"Maybe," agreed Eve. She was leaning against him, her good arm tucked into his elbow, so she had to lean up to whisper in his ear. "I was wondering what would happen if I just started kissing you…like this."

She nuzzled his ear, placing a light kiss on his neck just below his earlobe. His unshaven beard was rough on her face.

"I can definitely help you with an answer to that question," he said gruffly. "I would return the favor by kissing you back, like this."

Somehow he turned and took her into his arms without hurting her injured shoulder. The kisses he placed on her face, her throat, and her lips were soft and so tender. She kissed him back in the same way, brushing her lips on his as if to find the most perfect spot. When she sighed, he pulled back to look at her.

She held his gaze, mesmerized by the passion she saw in his eyes. "Thank you for rescuing me. I truly don't know what I would have done—"

Her words were cut off by Hill's lips on hers. Gentle at first to match hers, he then deepened the kiss, like a thirsty man for water.

"I've wanted to do this for days," he whispered. "You've no idea how much I wanted to pull you into my arms and cover you with kisses and then just hold you close and never let you go." He started all over again, tenderly touching her lips, already pink and plump from his kisses. "You are all I thought of on my way here. I was frantic that Jones would get to you before I could find you."

He set her away from him so he could look into her eyes. "And then I get here and find you gone. Out in the wilderness all alone… I think I was holding my breath until I saw you up on the cliff. And then I just wanted to rush up there and throw you over my shoulder. Oh, God… And then when you fell…"

Hill closed his eyes, thinking again of that horrible moment when he could do nothing but watch Eve tumble over the edge. He leaned his forehead against hers. "I thought you were dead," he whispered.

Eve waited for a long minute and then kissed him lightly on the lips. With her index finger, she traced the creases that worry had made on his brow. "Well, I'm not dead," she whispered back. "I'm almost entirely whole and very much alive, and I want you."

Hill kissed her softly on her injured shoulder and suddenly she couldn't get enough of him. Reaching up, she put her good arm around his neck and pulled his face closer to her lips. She placed featherlight kisses everywhere—on his brow, on his cheeks, and then on his lips—first his bottom lip, then the top one, and then… She could feel him catch his breath as she traced the line between his lips with the tip of her tongue, pressing her lips more firmly against his and willing him to take her offering even as he held her tight. He answered by meeting her tongue with his, gently exploring her mouth as their tongues tangled together.

At some point, Hill took control of their kiss, filling it with the desire he'd been denying for so long. His grip on her was almost crushing, and she started to understand the agony he'd been through when he watched her fall.

His tongue slipped between her lips and found hers again as he pulled her closer. Breathless, he finally broke the kiss, and whispered in her ear, "Eve, I desperately want to make love to you. May I?"

Nodding slowly, Eve gave her permission. Knowing in her heart that this might be the one and only time she could give in to her passion, she intended to make the very most of it. She would tell him about her father tomorrow.

Chapter 25

Hill had no intention of asking twice.

Even as Eve nodded her agreement, he was laying her gently down on the thick palette before the flames. The man's shirt that she wore with her breeches fell into a vee that pointed the way between her breasts. It was there that he started kissing her, working his way back up to her lips. He nipped at her full bottom lip and then thrust his tongue in to find hers. He groaned as she swirled her tongue into his mouth, mimicking his own explorations.

Trailing kisses back up to her ear, he whispered, "I want to see you, Eve. Please let me see you now."

Her shirt was made of a soft muslin that she wore over her chemise. Careful not to jar her injured shoulder, he gingerly gathered the soft material so that he could pull it over her head. Then he tenderly kissed his way back down her throat to the top of the chemise she still wore.

The fine lawn did almost nothing to hide nipples that were already dark and aroused. When wet, the material was like a thin skin that teased him, keeping him from his goal. He tried to suck, but could only lave the tip of her breast with his tongue, encouraging the nipple to an even harder point. As he covered her breasts with his palms and massaged them, he could feel her nipples becoming fuller and the tips hardening further. He kneaded gently and Eve arched her back in pleasure, teasing him by bringing herself closer to his hungry lips.

Hill untied the pink satin ribbon at the top of her chemise and opened the garment wide, exposing her completely. The heat from the flames gave her a rosy glow, but was only partially responsible for the blush that spread up and over her full, beautifully bare breasts to her throat and cheeks. The dark rose nipples puckered in the cold, and Eve started to cover herself. But Hill quickly captured her wrist and moved it over her head, with the effect of pushing her breasts even closer to his mouth and lips and tongue. Leaning forward as he held her arm immobile, he licked and then blew gently, first on one nipple and then the other, watching them rise again under his touch.

Then softly, softly, he touched the tip of his tongue to the tip of one breast. Her heart stopped and then with a great thump started again as she moaned and called his name, willing him to repeat the kiss on her other side. He plucked at the tip of first one breast and then the other with his thumb and finger, rolling each point gently to increase the sensation as Eve gasped her pleasure. In a swift movement, Hill captured the first nipple in his mouth and suckled—gently at first and then as Eve moaned, drawing harder.

"Please, Hill," she whispered as he paused to admire the picture she made.

"Please, what? What would you like me to do?"

"You know…"

"I do, but I want to hear you say it," said Hill blowing gently on one wet tip.

"Please keep doing what you were doing. Don't stop."

"Don't stop what? I want you to say the words."

"I want to feel your mouth on my breasts, Hill. Please?"

"It would be my very great pleasure, my lady."

He took her breasts again, suckling first one nipple and then the other, smiling as she writhed beneath him.

Then he trailed a finger down between her breasts and over her belly, slowly grinding his fully aroused erection against her. She instinctively opened her legs wider, and he smiled down at her. "Tell me if you like this part," he said as he moved his hand down to her thigh and caressed between her legs. She was still wearing her breeches, and the smooth material let him feel her heat as he rubbed between her legs.

"I do," she sighed. "Perhaps you would like it too?"

Mirroring his movements, Eve ran her thumb down the hard ridge in the front of his breeches. He sucked in his breath at the sensation and felt himself swell, straining at the already snug fit of the fabric. Helping himself to the buttons at the front of Eve's loose-fitting trousers, Hill slipped one hand inside to find the tangle of soft red curls at the apex of her legs. He played with those curls, wrapping them around his long finger and feeling the silken softness as he fingered her soft folds. Moving his hand slightly, he stroked down to find her opening and the heat between her legs.

Eve gasped at the new sensation, but it was Hill who groaned. "My god, Eve. You're so wet. I want to make you come now, my love. Can you feel me stroking you?"

In answer, Eve arched against his hand as he circled the sensitive folds that surrounded her hot core. Dipping his finger into her heat, he stroked her over and over. Eve had a grip on his arm, as if she were afraid he was going to stop. His finger went deeper, circling and stroking and mirroring the rhythm of her hips beneath him. Feeling her clinch around his finger, he whispered, "That's right, my love. You're almost ready."

"Hill, that feels so…so good. But I can't… I want to get there, but I don't know how. I don't know what to do."

"Let me do it, darling. Just relax and feel me touching you."

He kissed her breasts and circled each nipple with his tongue. A flush heralded Eve's climax and he watched the pink flush spread across her chest. "That's it, my love. You're almost there. Stay with me, Eve."

He pushed his finger deep inside her and, with a firmer stroke, circled and stroked again until Eve shouted his name and dissolved into pure, hot pleasure. Shuddering, she buried her face in his chest and he carefully wrapped her in his arms, vowing he would never let her go again.

****

After a minute or two, Eve took a deep breath. Her heartbeat was almost back to normal and she opened her eyes to look up at Hill. She leaned up to kiss him softly on the lips. "That was… I…" She took another deep breath and smiled. "Can we do it again?"

You greedy girl!" teased Hill. "So, you enjoyed that?"

She nodded.

"Good. Because we are going to do it again. But this time on the bed." He carried her to the small bed in the corner nearest the fire and laid her down gently. He followed her down and kissed her deeply, tasting and teasing her as he pressed himself against her. The way she moved beneath his hands made him harder than he'd ever been before.

"Is this what you want?" he asked. "Eve? Answer me or I'll stop. Is this what you want?"

"Yes! I mean, no… Oh, Hill, it's lovely, but this time I want you to be with me."

"I'm with you now. Here, let me show you." He put the tip of his tongue on her breast and she took a deep breath at the sensation.

"No, that's not what I mean, and you know it."

Hill furrowed his brow. "Eve, I don't know if—"

"Please, Hill. I want you so much." She touched his wrinkled brow and then gently pulled his face down to hers. "Please?" she whispered. "I want you inside me when I…you know…"

"Are you sure, Eve? I can make you come again, and we can wait for the rest until after we're married." He started kissing her breasts again.

"That's so lovely, Hill." She stroked his hair as he moved to her second breast. "But when you do that, I can't think, and I…"

"Good. Don't think, just feel. Feel me taking you up again like this…and this…and this."

In response, Eve pulled him down for a passionate kiss, tangling her tongue with his and pressing her lips hard against his. After a minute or so, she leaned back and took a breath. "Yes, your grace. I liked it a great deal," she said in a whisper. "And I would very much like to do it again, but this time I want you with me, inside me. I want you to feel the pleasure too."

"It's enough right now for me to give this to you, Eve. I don't have to—" His words turned into a groan as

Eve slipped one hand beneath the waist of his breeches. He was already rigid with desire, and as she stroked him, he felt himself growing bigger.

"Why should you do all the giving? I want to make you feel as wonderful as you've made me feel." Her hand continued its motion as she whispered to him. "Am I doing it right?" Abruptly she stopped.

"Yes, yes. You're doing it right, Eve. Just don't stop."

"I want to see you. I'm practically naked and you're almost fully dressed. I want to see the man who's going to make love to me. All of him."

"Very well," agreed Hill. "That seems only fair. Tell me what you want me to do."

"Really," said Eve with a wicked smile. "And you'll do it? No questions asked?"

"I will if you will," he replied with a smile. "Ladies first." He propped himself up on an elbow while he awaited his instructions.

"Take off your shirt so I can see what I've bargained for."

"I don't know that you'll be able to see much," said Hill as he pulled his shirt off over his head and tossed it at the foot of the bed. In the firelight, his skin looked like burnished gold, and when she reached out to caress his broad shoulders it was like stroking iron covered in satin. She never wanted to stop exploring the hard planes and angles of his back and the dark, silky hair on his chest. Oh, how she wanted this man.

"Now, take off the rest of your clothes," she ordered.

Hill quickly complied, divesting himself of his stockings and then his breeches. As he turned back to her, she couldn't help staring.

"Oh, my goodness, Hill…are you sure that we can…I mean what if things don't…er, um…fit when we…"

Hill had been watching her as his stiff member sprang free, and he chuckled at the look on her face. He crawled back up beside her on the bed and kissed her on the ear, whispering, "I promise everything will fit. There will be a little pain the first time, but we'll make it as little as possible—that is if you're still sure you want to do this now?"

Eve reached over and ran her hand tentatively up and down his rigid flesh, exploring his hot velvet skin. When he groaned, she furrowed her brow. "Hill, I'm so sorry! Am I hurting you?"

"You're doing it exactly right, but let me help you." He took her hand and guided her up and down his hard length. This time when he groaned, she smiled.

"Does that feel good?" she asked quietly.

"Oh, God, Eve. You have no idea how good it feels."

"So groaning is good? Or should I stop?"

"Yes! No! Groaning—at least this kind of groaning—is good. And no…please don't stop. In fact, you can do it even harder." He guided her hand faster up and down his length with more pressure and closed his eyes at the sensation. "That's right. Oh, Eve, that feels so wonderful."

"And what about here?" asked Eve, gently cupping and massaging him at the base of his erection.

Hill let out another groan. "Wherever did you learn to do that, my lady?" He opened his eyes and looked suspiciously at Eve.

"It feels good when you stroke me in other places. I

thought I would try the same on you. Do you mind?"

"Not in the least," said Hill, between gritted teeth.

Hill put his hand on top of hers and helped her with the long, hard strokes that had him moving his hips to her rhythm. When she stopped abruptly, his heart skipped a beat. Was he going too fast? Oh, God, if she wanted him to stop now, could he? He would have to. He would have to do what she wanted.

And then she was touching him again. He closed his eyes as she covered his entire length with firm, steady strokes. She stopped for a moment to explore the tip of him with curious fingers and delicate strokes that threatened his control. When she found beads of moisture there, she used them to lubricate her intimate massage of him. His groan of pleasure came from deep in his soul and he stilled her hand, closing his eyes and breathing a deep breath.

After a long moment, he opened his eyes and smiled. "My turn," he said.

"What?"

On his knees, Hill kissed his way all the way down her body, exploring her and tasting her. He stopped to lavish special attention on her breasts that tasted like the honeysuckle scent she wore. Hill had a wicked moment where he pictured dripping drops of fragrant honey onto her nipples and then sucking them off as she moaned and moved beneath him. Vowing to revisit that particular scenario on their honeymoon, he resumed his journey.

With his tongue, he traced a path up the inside of one thigh, higher and higher. He could feel Eve holding her breath as he moved to her opening and with the tip of his tongue touched the tight bud at her center. She gasped and tried to pull away, but he held her thighs firmly as he swirled his tongue around that one spot. She felt a dampness between her legs and when Hill put two fingers where his tongue had been, he pushed them deep into her hot wetness and started to stroke her as before.

"You're very wet, my love—that tells me how much you want me. You make me so hard—that's how you know how much I want you." He took himself in his hand and positioned himself at her opening. Eve tensed for the pain that she knew would come, but instead of invading her, he stroked her with his member, teasing and distracting her as he pulled her slowly toward another climax. He then pressed himself into her hot, wet passage, going deeper until he met the anticipated barrier. He withdrew almost entirely and then kissed her deeply, thrusting his tongue past her lips as he thrust himself deeply all the way inside her.

When she cried out, Hill replied, "I'm here, Eve. Just relax, my love, and let me hold you. The pain will pass in a moment, I promise."

Hill held himself deep inside, letting her adjust to the new fullness she felt. He kissed her and plucked gently at her nipples. When he felt her begin to relax, he started moving with a slow rhythm that he echoed with his kisses and his tongue.

He reached one finger down between them, slipping it between her legs to stroke the swollen bud. She tightened around him and he increased his thrusting. She immediately caught his rhythm and joined him as he thrust deeper, harder, and faster, taking them both higher and higher. All of a sudden, Eve called out his name and he felt her contract around him. She shuddered and seemed to let go as she fell over the very edge of pleasure. Holding her hips, he thrust again, and then again. And then, with a loud groan he pushed all the way in to the hilt and held himself deep inside her as he found his thunderous release.

Chapter 26

Hill was already up when Eve awoke. The kettle was heating over a merry fire and the room was toasty warm.

"How are you feeling?" The loaded question reflected Hill's concern—about her shoulder, about her fall, but most of all about their lovemaking the night before. It had occurred to him that she had been in a state of exhaustion—perhaps even shock. He had been so focused on making sure that he made her first time easy and wonderful that he'd not thought that he might have been taking advantage of her vulnerable state.

Eve's smile removed any guilt and any doubt from his mind. "I feel wonderful. A little sore—in all kinds of places—but that's to be expected, right?"

"I'm afraid it is, my love. I'm sorry if I was too exuberant in my lovemaking. I was—"

Eve's blushed. "Not about that, silly!" Her laugh was a beautiful sound. "Although now that you mention it, I might be a bit sore there as well." She laughed again. "I was talking about my shoulder and about how I must have hit every part of my body when I fell."

"Perhaps the doctor in town can give you some liniment to help the soreness and bruising. We can ask him when he looks at your shoulder. I have tea, and the toast is almost ready. I'll start packing things up so we can leave as soon as you're ready. Do you need help getting dressed?"

"Leave? What do you mean, leave?" Eve frowned up at him as she found her shirt and pulled it over her head with her good arm. "I haven't finished getting all the measurements I need for this area. I'll need at least two more days—maybe more, depending on what kind of assistant you are."

"Eve, I thought I had made myself clear. Jones is after us…is after *you.* You've been injured and need to see a doctor, and I'd really prefer that you spend a few days resting before we travel back to Tanglewood. Not to mention that in light of what happened last night, you and I will need to take a small detour to Gretna Green."

Who was this man and what had happened to her playful, generous, considerate lover of last night?

With one hand, Eve maneuvered herself into the breeches that had been hastily discarded the night before. She blushed bright pink as she remembered how he had struggled to pull them off her and what that struggle had ultimately led to. Standing up at her full height, she put her good hand on her hip.

"*You'd* prefer? The last time I looked, this was *my* expedition and *I'd* prefer to continue gathering the information I need for my map. My shoulder is feeling better. I can still draw and do calculations, and I can still take the measurements I need."

"Eve…"

"Perhaps you're not aware, your grace, but the King himself commissioned this work. It has already taken longer than it should have because of my father's death. I will not allow any more delays."

Hill narrowed his eyes. "You do realize I could throw you over my shoulder and carry you back to town. Then tie you to a horse and return you to London?"

"I know that you could *try* to do that. I also know what to do with unwanted advances from gentlemen, if you will recall." Eve couldn't help smiling at the involuntary movement from Hill that showed he did, in fact, remember their first meeting and how she had dropped him to the ground with one swift knee to his family jewels.

"Very well, let me ask you this: how do you propose to finish your work if you can't even set up your equipment?"

Eve stopped and looked at the instruments she had so easily carried into the woods yesterday morning. He was right. If she couldn't use both of her arms, then there was no way she would be able to carry and set up the equipment. "I may require an assistant. You have no experience, but since my choices are limited, I suppose you will have to do."

"You want *me* to be your assistant? You want the Duke of Camberton to follow you around, hauling equipment and recording numbers that you call out to me?"

Eve smiled. "Good! You seem to have grasped the concept well enough. That is an excellent start. I feel certain you will pick things up quickly as we go along, and, of course, I will tell you how to do everything. There's only a day, maybe two, of work left—although with your inexperience, it will most likely take longer."

Hill's face was truly comical.

"Or," Eve continued as she turned and walked back toward the table, "I suppose I could just stay here and wait until my arm is mended. That shouldn't take more than a week or two. And then I could do everything myself."

"I did tell you that I am under strict orders to bring you back to London at the earliest possible opportunity, did I not? What do you suggest I tell Whit?"

"You can tell him whatever you like, can't you? It's not like I'll be there to contradict whatever you say."

"Time is of the essence, Eve. Every minute we are out here alone, we are sitting ducks for Jones."

"We can easily see anyone who makes an advance on the mountain."

"Really? You didn't see me until I literally touched you on the shoulder and announced myself."

"You mean until you pushed me over the edge of the cliff?"

"For the last time, Eve, I didn't push you! I regret that I startled you, and I will always regret that you were injured in the fall, but you're obviously somewhat accident-prone. You probably would have stumbled and fallen by yourself and been out there all alone with no one to care for you."

"Is that what you're doing now? Caring for me? Because if you are, you're doing a terrible job of it! I don't feel very cared for at all!"

Eve was struggling to keep back tears. Her shoulder hurt from getting dressed, and it was seeming less and less likely that she would be able to finish her father's work. To top it all off, she had not told Hill the truth about Jones being her father. Would he leave her immediately once she told him? Now her tears truly threatened to betray her.

Hill considered the woman he loved as she stood in front of him. For someone so small, she exuded a powerful force—at least most of the time. But right now, she was vulnerable. He could see the pain on her face and the tears in her eyes and still she argued with him. Standing up for what she wanted and for what she needed, and making her case in spite of all the odds. She frustrated him more than anyone else he'd ever known. But the thing was, right now, all he really wanted to do was wrap her carefully in his arms, cover her with kisses, and make everything right for her.

Unfortunately, it was probably the last thing Eve wanted right now.

Briefly he wondered to himself if there would ever be a time when Eve would do as he asked without questioning him.

Probably not. Perhaps another approach might be in order.

Coming up behind her, Hill leaned forward to kiss the back of her neck, "Eve, I don't want to argue with you. I'm only worried for your safety."

He turned her around in his arms and took her lips in a slow, passionate kiss.

His tender kiss made her ache everywhere for his touch. Eve could feel her body reacting as it remembered all the delicious things that went with kisses like that, and, for a moment, she gave in.

And then she returned his kiss. She let her passion go unchecked, mindlessly pressing herself against his chest as she leaned into him. After a few more moments of this most wonderful kissing, she stepped back, taking a deep breath.

And then another.

She was glad to see his eyes dark with the same passion she felt. And she noticed—with some satisfaction—that his breeches were pulled tight over a rather impressive bulge.

Hill looked at her and raised an eyebrow. "What was that?"

"What was what?"

"That... That... What was that you did just now?"

Eve wrinkled her brow. "I'm not sure I know what you mean, my love." She looked up at Hill with an innocent face. "Oh, wait. Do you mean using kisses to get my way? But surely that would be an unfair way to win an argument—don't you agree?"

Hill narrowed his eyes at her and then raised that one eyebrow. "Well played, madam. Well played. And I will stipulate that it is perhaps not always the *best* way to advance my cause. However, I do reserve the right to use kisses—and other, similar enticements—in any way necessary to change your mind should we ever disagree in the future."

"And you think simply declaring it like that makes it acceptable?"

Hill smiled and nodded, and Eve found herself laughing in spite of herself. "Very well. As long as you allow me the same right to use whatever womanly wiles I can come up with to get you to agree with my way of thinking or do what I want you to do."

"Done," said Hill. "So, where do we start my apprenticeship?"

Chapter 27

Two days had flown by. Working as a team, Eve and Hill had made progress that exceeded her most optimistic expectations. As it turned out, having a smart, willing duke as an assistant was an excellent idea and having a pair of muscled arms and a strong back to lug all of the ungainly equipment up hill and down was definitely a plus. Not to mention that having the company of a handsome, attentive, entertaining man was a delightful, and unexpectedly arousing, benefit—a fact that made Eve blush every time she acknowledged it.

The unseasonably warm weather—because of the Gulf Stream, Eve explained—had continued up until today. But this morning, a storm loomed on the southwest horizon, and they worked quickly to pack up and start the trek back to the village.

"How is your shoulder?"

Eve stopped packing with a guilty start and grinned. "I didn't even notice it," she said. "That's good, right?"

"It is," he agreed. Smiling, he placed a kiss on her lips and drew her into his arms. "I still think you need to be careful with it, but I'm very glad you're feeling better."

"Thank you for being such a good sport. It really helped to have you here. I wouldn't be anywhere near finished if I were doing it alone—even if my shoulder was fine."

"So now what do you do? What do you do with all the information your worthy assistant helped you gather?"

"Next comes the fun part—at least for me. I do all sorts of calculations—mostly geometry to triangulate the measurements and figure out the coordinates for latitude and longitude. And then I plot their location on my map."

"I had no idea so much math was involved."

"It's fun," said Eve. "Here, I'll show you." She sat down at the small table and quickly did a series of calculations, writing down the results in her journal. "See, all of that just to get to these coordinates."

"But aren't map coordinates written in degrees, minutes, and seconds? Those are just regular numbers with decimal places."

"I leave them as decimal numbers to make the calculations easier. If I wanted to give a location to someone, I would probably convert them to degrees, minutes, and seconds—like this. It's more obvious and makes more sense to people."

"So maybe they *are* coordinates!"

"What are you talking about?" Eve looked puzzled.

"You remember I told you about the papers I found in Glenly's valise?" Hill was patting his pockets. "And I told you that one of the papers had women's names along with a rough sketch and some numbers?"

"Yes, I remember."

"The numbers are long decimal numbers. They look like the numbers you wrote before you translated them to degrees, minutes, and seconds. I think they are the decimal numbers for map coordinates."

"Do you have the numbers?"

"Yes, here they are. I left the original for Whit, but

I made a copy. I wanted to see if I could figure out what the numbers meant. I thought about map coordinates, but when I translated them into degrees, minutes, and seconds and plotted them on a map, they landed me somewhere in the Bristol Channel. But maybe I made a mistake." Hill handed Eve a piece of folded paper with a sketch and some numbers on it. "What do you think?"

Eve quickly converted the decimal numbers into degrees, minutes, and seconds so she could plot their location. She shook her head. "You didn't make a mistake. I get the same thing—if they are map coordinates, they take you to the Bristol Channel. Could the numbers be encoded in some way?"

"I suppose so. I think Whit was going to have Vivian look at them as soon as he—Eve, what's wrong?"

Eve had turned the paper over and was looking at the names on the other side. Her face had turned ashen. "These names," she whispered. "What are these names?"

"These are the names I was telling you about. The women who are on Jones's list. Whit believes—actually, we all believe—that these are the women Jones has targeted. Obviously there's Vivian and Linney, and then you. I think the others—Rose, Jenny, and Deborah—are names of women who work for Whit—possibly in Paris. I don't know why the name Jenny has a line through it. It's possible that—"

"Hill, Deborah is my mother's name! Jones is going after my mother!"

Chapter 28

The trip back to Blackberg was a blur. Eve barely remembered explaining to Nancy and to Mrs. Findlay why she would not be taking the carriage but would instead be riding with Hill. Alone.

There was simply no time to tell them that the very circumstance about which they were all so concerned had already happened. Eve was unwilling to announce an engagement that she knew would not stand after Hill learned the identity of her natural father, so she asked Hill to keep their plans private, but she couldn't help a small smile as she recalled the activities that had led to that promise—a smile which didn't go unnoticed by Mrs. Findlay.

When Eve saw Mrs. Findlay pull Hill aside for a private chat, she was burning with curiosity. Once they were on the road back to Tanglewood, she said to Hill, "What was that all about? Mrs. Findlay was talking your ear off! She seemed very intense, and you looked like a little boy who got caught with his finger in the pie."

Hill choked on her description and then laughed. "You're not that far off," he admitted. "She was suggesting that we spend tonight at the Anvil Inn in Gretna Green," said Hill. "After saying our vows, of course. She said she understood that you wanted to get back to your mother as soon as possible, but that your mother wouldn't want her only daughter's reputation ruined because of her. And then she gave me very clear directions. And a map."

In spite of—or perhaps because of—all the tension, Eve started laughing. "According to Nancy, Mrs. Findlay can be very determined when she sets her mind on something. What did you say?"

"I agreed with her and promised to do just that. The turn we need to take is about a mile down this road."

Eve's mouth was open, but no sound came out. Her horse kept following Hill's mount, so they were almost at the turn in the road to Gretna Green before she could even speak. "Hill! What do you mean you promised? You promised to do what?"

"Marry you before we spend the night at the Anvil Inn. We have to stay somewhere tonight. Gretna Green is only about five miles out of our way."

"I can't believe you would say something like that to poor Mrs. Findlay. I don't like the idea of lying to her."

Hill stared at Eve for a minute. "I never lie," he said, "and I never, *ever* break a promise."

"So, what are you saying? Are you saying that we're going to be married? Today? This afternoon?"

"We should be there in about two hours," confirmed Hill. "You said you would marry me, remember?"

"Of course I remember," snapped Eve. "I just didn't think that you meant today."

"What difference does it make? Have you changed your mind?"

"What? Of course not. I just… Well, I didn't think it would be so… I don't…" How could she tell him that he was the one who would most likely be looking for a way out of their agreement. "Do *you* still want to marry me? When you proposed, we were both under a great deal of stress. I don't want to have a marriage where you feel as if you were forced into marrying me."

"Of course I want to marry you, Eve. I've asked you twice now and I've known that we should be together from the moment I met you—well, perhaps not that very first moment, but definitely later that day. The time we spent together over the summer just made me realize how much I loved you and wanted to be with you. And now, after the last few days…I want us to be married now. I don't want to wait. If I hadn't had to go on the mission for Whit, I think we would already be married."

Eve couldn't think of anything to say. She had less than an hour to come up with a reason they couldn't get married or else Hill would be her husband by dinnertime. And once Hill found out that the notorious Monsieur Jones had seduced her mother and was Eve's natural father—ugh, she could *not* think of the man that way—Hill would want to be as far away from her as he could possibly be.

For a brief moment, Eve considered not telling him. Hill was the one insisting on a quick wedding. Wasn't one of the dangers of such haste the fact that there might be things they did not know about each other? But that wouldn't be fair, and, like as not, he would come to resent her for not telling him the truth before she married him. Even an annulment would cause a scandal throughout the *ton*. Eve wasn't even sure they could get an annulment, because technically they had already consummated the marriage. And from the look in Hill's eyes, tying up that particular loose end was high on his list of tonight's evening activities. Besides, she loved him. She would not start a marriage with a huge lie. There would never be any trust between them if she did.

She had to tell him. She'd hoped for a more suitable time, but perhaps this was for the best. Was there ever a suitable time to tell the man you loved that your father, a notorious spy and traitor to his country, was the man trying to kill him?

Eve stifled a giggle and then a sob. The man she loved. He would never be hers now. Once he knew her ancestry, she would be lucky if he even escorted her back to her mother. She would never regret the time they had spent together, and she'd never forget how he made love to her so tenderly. Eve brushed angrily at the tear running down her cheek.

Knowing Hill, he would try to say that since he'd taken her virginity he had an obligation. If he was concerned about her reputation after their afternoon in the castle ruins, surely spending three days alone with him in the wilderness would take care of any reputation she had left after word got out that Jones was her father.

"Eve, what's wrong? Are you upset that we're not going to have a big wedding?"

Eve seized on that idea. She could say that. She could say that she wanted a big wedding just like Avery and Linney had. She could say that she wanted her mother at her wedding and her cousin who had inherited the title when her father died. She could say all of that—

Except none of it was true.

She didn't want a big wedding. She didn't want her mother there. The only person other than Hill that she would want there would be her father—her real father, Lord Tangier, who had loved her as his own. And he was gone. Tears came expectedly.

"Please don't cry, my love. I don't want you to be unhappy. If you want a big wedding, we can wait. As long as we don't wait too long. Eve, the only reason I allowed myself to make love to you was because I knew we were going to be married. I never would have taken your virginity otherwise. I have a sister, Eve. I know how people talk and I understand what a precarious situation I've put you in, but if you don't want to get married here, we can do it in London or at Haversham House or wherever you want. It doesn't matter to me when or where, as long as I'm marrying you. I love you and I want—"

"Monsieur Jones is my father."

"What?"

"Please. Don't say anything until I get it all out, or I will never be able to say it. I didn't want to tell you because I know it will change how you feel about me, and I love you so much. Imagine a duke of the realm being married to the daughter of Napoleon's spymaster." She tried to smile, but her heart was breaking.

"It's laughable," Eve continued, "except that it's not at all funny. When Linney told me what she had overheard, I confronted my mother and she finally admitted that she'd been unfaithful to Lord Tangier on her wedding night and that I was the result of that liaison." Eve talked faster and faster as she searched her pockets for her handkerchief. When Hill handed her his, she stopped and sighed. Taking the pristine square of linen, she hung her head. She couldn't bear to see the look on his face.

Clutching at the few shreds of dignity she had left, she started again. "I love you, Hill. I love you so very much. I think I've loved you ever since we met at the inn. But I love you enough to know that you cannot be married to someone like me—someone whose bloodline is tainted by a traitor. I only ask that you help me get back to Tanglewood so I can make sure that my…my father doesn't kill my mother. Hopefully he will soon be arrested and hanged."

Tears started down her face again and she dabbed at her eyes with Hill's handkerchief. "I'm so sorry, Hill. I'm so very, very sorry."

She didn't dare look at him. He didn't say a word, and she could almost feel the horror and disgust, the anger and the disappointment. His silence was worse than any angry accusations. She was glad she'd finally told him the truth, but this was horrible. Finally, she couldn't stand it any longer and looked up at him. He was watching her. She had never seen him look so angry.

"Are you finished?" he asked.

Unable to speak, Eve just nodded.

"I am extremely disappointed, Eve."

Eve hung her head. A tear squeezed out of her tightly shut eyes. She couldn't begin to imagine what her life was going to be like without him. Even during the times when she had been furious with him, some part of her had hoped that they could find each other again. And now they had—only to be separated because of something neither of them had any control over. She tried to listen to his words of censure.

"As I just told you and as I thought you knew, I *never* break my promises. As a result, I don't make many. But those I do make, I keep. Always. I asked you to marry me. I asked you to live with me and love me and be my wife and my duchess and eventually the mother of my children. And I promised that I would love and cherish you for all the days we had together. Why in the world would you think that I would break the most important promise I'd ever made in my life?"

"But Hill, my father is—"

"Viscount Glenly. Yes, I know. Avery told me when I returned to Haversham House from Glenhaven. We had wondered what Jones' connection to your mother was when he went through the tunnel to her room. It doesn't surprise me that he seduced your mother—although, I must say, it also would not have surprised me to learn that your mother seduced him."

"But Hill, he's Napoleon's spymaster. And you and Whit said that he was insane."

"Yes, and if Napoleon—God forbid—should ever escape Saint Helena, I don't expect you to volunteer to take up Monsieur Jones' position with the emperor. As far as the madness goes, I think Jones—or Glenly or whatever you want to call him—has driven himself mad with his own actions. He is an evil man, there's no doubt about that. Just as there's no doubt about the fact that you are not. Eve, Jones may be your natural father, but your real father—the man who raised you and cared for you and loved you until the day he died—was Lord Tangier. He's the only father you've ever known and the only father you have ever needed. If he were still alive, I would insist that we be married in a big church wedding just so he could have the honor of walking you down the aisle. I think if he were here today, the thing he would want most is for his daughter to be safe and loved and happy. I happen to think the best way to accomplish that is for us to be married. Today. However…"

Eve cocked her head and looked at Hill. He was obviously struggling with a decision. Finally, he reached over and took her hand and brought it to his lips.

"However, I'm releasing you from your promise to

marry me."

Eve's eyes opened wide. This was not what she wanted! "Hill, no! I—"

He shook his head. "Let me finish," he said quietly. "I release you from your promise so you can be free from any guilt or shame or regret or whatever it is that you're feeling. I want you to make a decision based on only one thing—what *you* want."

Eve nodded, tears filling her eyes. She knew what she wanted. She'd known it all along. She wanted to be with Hill for the rest of her life. She wanted to tease him and console him and make love to him until they were both breathless. She wanted to be his lover, his friend, and his wife, and she wanted him to be her husband.

They were on the outskirts of town. Hill dismounted and wrapped his horse's reins around the low branch of a nearby tree. He took the reins for Eve's mare and wrapped them around the same branch. Then he reached up to help Eve dismount. Holding her hand in his, he went down on one knee before her.

"And now, Lady Genevieve, I have a question to ask you. Again. Will you make me the happiest of men and do me the honor of becoming my wife?"

Looking into those eyes that were dark and almost black with passion, Eve took a breath. "I will on one condition, your grace."

Hill raised an eyebrow at her. "And what condition might that be, my lady?"

"That you marry me this afternoon so that I might have my wedding night tonight."

Hill grinned and kissed the palm of her hand. "I believe that can be arranged, but I suggest we push on. The night comes early this far north."

****

They had made love twice already—the first with an almost frantic wonderment and disbelief that they were actually married and then again slowly, leisurely, with Hill tapping his extensive experience to give Eve the wedding night she deserved. They had slept then, but now, as the sun was rising, Eve felt the stirring of desire again. Wanting to wake him gently, she toyed with the dark hair on his broad chest and then said, "Did you know that we would actually say our vows over an anvil at the blacksmith shop?"

Already awake, Hill had been savoring the feeling of having a beautiful woman, warm from his loving, naked in his arms upon waking. Now he captured her hand and held it still lest he be distracted by the playful movements of her fingers and give in to wanting her again.

"Not having ever been married—at Gretna Green or anywhere else—I must say that I did not," he replied. "According to the blacksmith, we didn't *have* to get married at the smithy, we just had to make our declaration in front of two witnesses. The blacksmith and his wife have done it so many times before that it was the easiest way. If we are blessed with any daughters in our future, we must remember how very easy this was and keep close watch over them."

Eve laughed. "Spoken like a true father. We haven't been married for even a day and you're already trying to figure out how to discipline our children."

"It is never too early to think ahead. Besides, there's always a chance that it could happen sooner rather than later. As you may have noticed, our…uh…conjugal activities have not involved any precautions that I might have normally taken."

Eve blushed to the tips of her ears. "I had not even thought about that! But you had?"

"Believe me when I say that I have always been very deliberate about that particular aspect of my…uh…my interactions. At least until recently, when I find that I have become quite careless."

"How recently," demanded Eve, tugging at his chest hair.

"*Very* recently," murmured Hill as he pulled her underneath him and proceeded to demonstrate how very careless he could be. He caught her wrist and stretched her arm up above her head, resting it on the pillow.

"Do not move your arm from that position or I will tie it there," he warned sternly as she started to cover herself. He held up his discarded neckcloth in one hand. "I mean it, Eve. Leave your arms where they are. I want to look my fill at my new wife." He smiled at the beautiful picture she made—her raised arms thrust her creamy breasts forward, tempting him with their darker, pointed tips. Flushed with warmth from the bedclothes, she smiled as he moved to exercise his husbandly rights once again.

Some time later, after that rather enthusiastic end to their wedding night, Hill lay snoring gently while Eve plastered herself to his chest, allowing not even a breath of air between them. She had almost lost him, she knew that. And she was determined that it would never, *ever* happen again.

****

The trip to Tanglewood from Gretna Green was

uneventful, but long. Knowing that Eve was exhausted from worry and that neither of them had slept much the night before, Hill insisted they take a carriage for the first leg of their journey, They stopped at an inn where Hill registered them as Mr. and Mrs. Barbour, not wanting to compel the attention—or the danger—that a duke and duchess traveling with only a coachman would attract.

Hill took a large room, but only one for the both of them. And even though she had already had *multiple* wedding nights, Eve was suddenly shy at the thought of spending a normal evening alone with the Duke of Camberton. When she tried to explain her feelings to her new husband, he grinned and was suddenly just Hill again.

"I was actually thinking the same thing," he confessed as he undid the hooks at the back of her gown. "Imagine me keeping company with the Duchess of Camberton!"

A knock on the door interrupted her relieved laughter and revealed several servants bearing a copper tub and buckets of steaming hot water.

"Can you manage the rest on your own?" he asked as the last servant exited the room. "I'm going down to see about procuring horses for us tomorrow. We need to get to Tanglewood faster. Do you think you can ride tomorrow?"

"Only if I can wear my breeches and ride astride," said Eve. "I'm in much too much of a hurry to ride sidesaddle."

"I can't think of a single reason to say no," said Hill with a twinkle in his eye, "and I can think of many, *many* reasons to say yes!"

By the time Hill returned, Eve had bathed, pulled on

her nightgown, and fallen fast asleep. Hill took a quick bath and joined her in bed. Cuddling up to her back, he put his arm around her waist and pulled her closer. Tonight he was content just to hold her in his arms.

****

Of course, they made much better time on horseback, but they were still forced to stop for the night. If the weather held, they would be at Tanglewood by early afternoon the next day. The dark gray sky threatened rain, but they saw only a few showers right after they started and soon outrode the storm.

"Hill, I've been thinking."

"That can't be good," said her husband.

Eve made a face at him but continued. "I was thinking about the numbers on that paper you found in Glenly's bag. I'm certain they're map coordinates."

"Even though they point to the middle of the Bristol Channel?"

"Could they be identifying a rendezvous point for two boats?"

"I suppose it's possible," said Hill. "But how does the sketch fit in? It's obviously a map of a village somewhere. Maybe it's the port town closest to the rendezvous point?"

They rode silently for a while. Periodically, the sun broke through the clouds to cast sunbeams onto the countryside, creating a series of rainbows that made Eve smile. No matter where she was, she could always find beauty in her surroundings. *No matter where she was*. Of course!

"Hill, what did you use as the prime meridian?"

"I beg your pardon?"

"When you mapped those numbers as coordinates, what was the location of your prime meridian? Where was the your zero longitude line?"

"Yes, I know what a prime meridian is. It goes through the Royal Observatory in London."

"So, you used the Greenwich Prime Meridian."

"Yes, of course."

"But Monsieur Jones—or Glenly—or whoever wrote that list and those numbers—wanted to communicate that information to *French* operatives and *French* troops, correct?"

"Yes, I would assume so. Most of the information we've intercepted has been in French."

"Then maybe those *are* map coordinates, but they're using the *Paris* Meridian, not the Greenwich Meridian."

"Of course! By God, Eve, you may have figured it out! I've already sent word to Whit to meet us at Tanglewood. I thought we could use some help if Jones is there. He'll want to know about this right away."

"Off the top of my head, if you used those coordinates with the Paris Meridian, they would put you just outside London. Somewhere to the southeast of the city."

Hill looked at her in astonishment.

"What?" she said.

"You never cease to amaze me, your grace. I think the Duke of Camberton is a very lucky fellow."

****

As they got closer to Tanglewood, Eve's apprehension grew. What would she find? If Jones had been there, would he have harmed her mother? The little she knew about the man did not allay her fears. Jones had proved himself over and over to be a brutal, ruthless killer. Eve had no reason to believe he would spare her mother simply because the two had been involved in a romantic affair in the past. If it even was in the past. If Eve was honest with herself, she had to admit that at least part of her worry was that her mother would join Jones and run away with him.

Putting those circling thoughts out of her head for the hundredth time, Eve looked over at Hill. He looked worried too. He raised his eyebrows in a question and when she smiled at him, he said, "We'll be there soon."

In less than an hour, Eve was pointing out the steeple of the church in the little village that had grown up outside of Tanglewood Manor and shared its name. Today, unlike other times she'd come home, Eve did not stop to visit the shops or greet the people who had been her extended family growing up. However, outside the inn at the end of the main road, a young boy and girl waved to flag them down.

"Lady Eve! Lady Eve!"

"Helen! Homer! How are you? How is your mother? Is everything all right?"

"It's Ma what told us to watch for you," said the boy. "She said you'd be here today or tomorrow."

"We're supposed to give you a message from our Da," said Helen. "He was up at the manor house doing some trimming and saw a man come to visit Lady Tangier all dressed up fancy. Da heard Mr. Yates tell the gentleman that Lady Tangier was not at home. That she had gone back to London, but the man pushed his way in and Mr. Yates was yelling at him and then everything was quiet. Da said to tell you that we'd not seen anyone from the house since—not Mr. Yates, not Cook, not any of the maids or footmen!"

"Where's Lord Tangier? Is he at the house as well?"

"His lordship is still away," said Homer. "Ma said he went back to his old house to look for a wife."

"You're not supposed to say that," said Helen, punching her brother in the arm. "Ma said."

"Ouch! Well, that's where he went and Lady Eve might want to know."

"Thank you, Homer. I did want to know. Do you know when he's coming back?"

"Da said not for another week," said Helen.

Eve looked at Hill. Her eyes were wide with fear. "I've got to go and find my mother," she said. "Heaven only knows what he's done with the servants."

"Homer, listen to me," said Hill. "I need you to do something for Lady Eve."

Homer looked to Eve for her approval.

"It's fine, Homer. This is the Duke of Camberton. He's a very good friend of mine."

Hill raised an eyebrow at Eve at her description of her new husband, but he let it stand for the moment. "Homer, go as quickly as you can and find your Da. Tell him to bring four men up to the house. Tell him not to let anyone at the house see them. They should go through and wait in the kitchen until they get a signal from Lady Eve."

Homer frowned.

"What's the matter, Homer?" asked Eve. "It's all right. You can do what His Grace said."

"Helen's faster," muttered the boy.

"What?"

Homer raised his head with a disgusted look on his face. "Helen's faster," he said clearly. "Da is working all the way over at the spring, and Helen is faster."

"Good man, Homer," said Hill. "Well said. Off you go then, Helen. Do you remember the message?"

"Yes sir, your grace," said Helen as she started down the road toward the spring.

"Homer, I have another task for you."

Homer straightened up like a wilted flower receiving water. "Yes, your grace?"

"There is another man coming to visit Tanglewood. You can call him Mr. Whit. He should be here later today. When you see him, tell him that Jones is up at the house and that Camberton and Lady Eve went up to find him. Have you got that?

"Yes, your grace! I'll tell him as soon as I see him."

"There might be others with him, but only give the message to Mr. Whit, do you understand?"

"Yes, your grace!"

"Come on, then," said Eve. "It's still another mile to the house."

As they rode up to the house, Eve and Hill made a plan. "I'll go in first," said Hill. "When it's safe, I'll call out to you."

"*That's* your plan? No. She's my mother, and as soon as we get there, I'm going in to find her. That's the plan."

"Eve, he could have a gun. Even if he only has a knife, if he's startled, he could harm you or your mother. It would be better to surprise him."

"Very well, I'll go and make sure that my mother is unharmed and then you can come in and surprise him. I live here. He'll be expecting me, so maybe he will let down his guard once he sees that I'm by myself."

"Or he'll be suspicious because you're alone."

"I'll tell him that my maid and footman are downstairs."

Hill sighed. He wasn't going to win this argument—at least not any time soon. "Very well, then. Go and find your mother. I'll follow you." It was the worst idea he'd ever heard of, but it was clear that Eve was going to do exactly what she said she was going to do.

"If he's in your mother's room, see if you can get him to turn his back to the door. I'll be outside the room for the chance to take him by surprise. Remember, *he* doesn't know that we know he's here."

They approached from the stables so that there were no windows from which someone could see them walking toward the house. Eve went first, making her way up to the main entry hall. Stealthily, Hill followed, staying in the shadows and hoping against hope that Jones wasn't completely mad.

"Mother? Mother, I'm back. Where are you? And where is Yates? Has everyone taken the afternoon off?"

Eve started up the steps that led to the family wing. "Mother? Yates?"

At the top of the steps, Eve turned toward her mother's rooms, calling out again as she walked down the hallway. "Mother, where are you? I'm starting to worry." Stopping in front of her mother's closed door, she knocked sharply.

"Mother?"

Before opening the door, Eve turned to make certain Hill was hidden from view.

"Eve, darling!" Her mother's voice came from her dressing room. "Eve, whatever are you doing here? Why didn't you tell me you were coming, dear?"

Relief flooded through Eve. Her mother was alive!

Jones obviously hadn't been here yet. She took a step inside the room. "Mother, what in the world is going on? Where is Yates and where are all the servants? I was worried about you! We travelled all the way from Blackwood to make sure you—"

"Eve, run!" Lady Tangier screamed. "Run!"

Eve could hear the sound of flesh hitting flesh and heard something being dragged. She ran into her mother's dressing room and stopped. Lady Tangier lay at an angle on the chaise longue in her dressing gown. Sitting beside her was a large, very strong-looking man with brown hair and a darker beard trimmed quite short. He was smiling up at Eve with a pleasant expression. In fact, the only thing objectionable about him was the knife he held to her mother's throat.

Eve screamed and the man stood up, jerking Lady Tangier to her feet with him. "Shut it," he growled. "Don't scream again or I swear I'll end her life right here."

Eve clamped a hand over her mouth as the man jerked Lady Tangier around in front of him. Eve couldn't help but notice the bruise forming on her mother's cheek. Her dressing gown had been pulled roughly over a torn nightgown.

"I think it's about time we met, Eve," said the man evenly. "I am Viscount Glenly, your father."

"My father?" Eve laughed. "You are not my father." Advancing slowly, she said, "Mother, are you all right? Did he hurt you?"

"I'm fine, darling, but you need to go. Please let her go, Phillip. You don't want to hurt her. She's your daughter."

"You're right, my love, I don't want to hurt dear

Eve. I simply want to use her to lure that fancy duke she has sniffing around her. Where is he, Eve? I know that a lady such as yourself did not travel alone. Where is the Duke of Camberton?"

"My goodness. You're rather behind in your gossip, aren't you? Have you not heard? The Duke of Camberton jilted me. He all but asked me to marry him when we were together this summer, and then he left. I heard nothing from him until I saw him again at my friends' wedding on New Year's Eve."

Glenly laughed. "Well, that's just one more reason to put a bullet through him. I will track him down and defend your honor, my dear. I'll challenge him to a duel because he played with the affections of my daughter. Come to think about it, the man has also played with the affections of my sister, so I have multiple reasons to demand satisfaction. And I won't be satisfied until the man is dead! Now tell me: where is Camberton?"

"I told you that I—"

"Do not toy with me, Eve. I will slit your mother's throat and then yours after that if you do not tell me where he is right now!"

"Let her go," said Eve. "Go now and you can still escape. The footman won't come up unless I call him."

"It's nice that you're looking out for your father, Eve," said Glenly. "I appreciate that. Unfortunately, I do not care to leave any witnesses who can identify me. Tell me where he is."

"I must first tend to my mother," said Eve, slowly moving toward the two. "She is injured. Your work, I presume? Can't you please let her go?"

Glenly looked as if he were considering her request and Eve took another step. Suddenly, he pushed Lady

Tangier. She fell heavily onto the chaise and screamed as Glenly grabbed Eve around the waist and put a knife to his daughter's throat.

Glenly laughed. "There! That's much better, isn't it? No one wants that bitch anymore. Certainly not me. But you, my dear, you remind me of how she used to look. She was a beauty when I first met her. Stop struggling, dear Eve. I've dealt with men who were far stronger than you. You are perhaps even more beautiful and, of course, you're worth a great deal more to me. You can help me get my revenge on the Ice Duke and his minions—including your dashing Camberton. Once they have been dealt with, then you will be my leverage to help me make my escape."

As Glenly rambled on and on, he got louder and louder. Eve kept struggling against him, keeping him moving around until at last his back was to the open door.

"You know you will never get away with it," she said. "They won't let you escape—not after everything you have done. You betrayed England for Napoleon, a nasty, stupid, tiny man with an even smaller reputation, who—"

"Enough!" Glenly was shouting now, his face purple with rage. "Napoleon is the greatest man who ever lived! He escaped Alba and he will escape Saint Helena and then he will rule the world!"

Just outside the door, Hill cursed softly to himself and willed Eve to stop baiting the man. He knew she was doing it as a distraction, but what if Glenly snapped and killed her?

"Once the Ice Duke and his lieutenants have been eliminated, I can return to being Viscount Glenly. Eventually I will return to court and, with any luck at all,

I'll be able to put an end to the fat old sot who sent that idiot Wellington to Waterloo. The world will then see how much they need a great leader and they will be begging for my emperor's return from Saint Helena."

Jones was still ranting and moving about when Lady Tangier suddenly put out her foot. He stumbled and the knife went flying. Before he could regain his balance, Eve turned and slammed her knee into his groin. Glenly doubled over and fell to the ground, but as he did, he grabbed Eve's ankle and pulled her down too. She sprawled on top of him and then scrambled to get up and away, but Glenly lunged for her, grabbing the arm she had recently injured and pulling her in front of him just as Hill charged into the room, kicking the knife out of Jones' reach.

"Ah, your grace. I knew you would be somewhere close by. How kind of you to call. You know my daughter, I believe, although I understand that you have been rather ungentlemanly in your conduct with her. As a matter of fact, I was under the impression that it was my sister you wanted to speak to me about, not my daughter."

"Let her go, Glenly," said Hill.

"My dear boy, that would be a rather stupid thing to do, would it not? Have you, in your pursuit of me over these many years, ever known me to be stupid?"

The sound of horses riding up drew Jones' attention for an instant. His grip on Eve loosened and she elbowed him in the gut just as Hill launched himself forward to punch him in the face. Staggering backwards, Jones pulled a dagger from his boot. With the strength and agility of a madman, he attacked Hill, plunging the knife into his side.

"Hill!" screamed Eve, rushing toward her husband. Jones grabbed her around the neck just as Hill, staggering from his wound, started toward Jones again.

"Take one more step and I swear I'll cut her," shouted Jones. He touched the razor-sharp knife to Eve's skin and a line of blood appeared on her throat. Hill froze.

Then, as if she'd fainted, Eve suddenly drooped in Jones' arms throwing him off balance. "Stand up," he screamed. Hill took advantage of the diversion and tackled Jones, freeing Eve from his grasp. A shot rang out. Jones stumbled forward and then fell to the floor with a thud.

Eve and Hill looked up to see a puff of smoke and Lady Tangier pointing a tiny, pearl-handled pistol at the unmoving man who lay bleeding all over her Aubusson carpet.

****

The commotion outside only intensified when Hill and Eve joined the fray.

The Duke of Whitley, along with Avery and Edgewood, had arrived just in time to hear the shot fired by Lady Tangier. As they raced toward the house, Eve and Hill descended the stairs—Eve searching frantically for someone to tend to Hill's wound while he was trying to find someone to tend her injured shoulder.

Edgewood finally sat both of them down in the kitchen and pronounced Hill lucky that the knife had missed anything important and then followed Hill's unusual yet clever instruction to wrap his weskit around Eve to keep her arm from further injury.

Lacey, Lady Tangier's maid, along with Mr. Yates

the butler, Cook, and Mrs. Appleton the housekeeper had been locked into the cold room. Once freed, they tended to Lady Tangier's bruises with cold compresses, anisette oil, and more than one snifter of brandy. Eve's mother was uncharacteristically quiet about her role in the afternoon's proceedings, and after telling Whit her side of the story only once, she pleaded a headache and retired to the guest room farthest from her boudoir.

Eve and Hill led Whit, Avery, and Edgewood up to Lady Tangier's suite to collect Glenly's body. They had discussed what story would need to be put out to explain the shooting death of a viscount whose family lines went back to William the Conqueror—a story that would not compromise any of the people or operations in Whit's vast network.

Hill opened the door to Lady Tangier's suite and Eve preceded him in. When she gasped, Hill came in quickly behind her. Before them was only a still-wet bloodstain on the carpet. There was no trace of Jones.

****

Hill called on the servants and the men from the village to search the grounds of Tanglewood, but they found nothing. Apart from the blood on the rug, the wound in Hill's side, and Lady Tangier's bruises, there was no trace that Glenly had ever been there.

"I shouldn't have left him alone unguarded," said Hill, running his hand through his hair in a familiar sign of frustration. But Eve was having none of it.

"You turned him over, Hill. My God, we all saw that he was dead. He wasn't breathing. And, as you might remember, you were bleeding all over the place."

"Don't beat yourself up, Camberton," said Whit.

"Jones has escaped from just about every situation imaginable. Edgewood swears the man drowned after he had kidnapped Vivian, and Avery was certain he landed a shot when they met in the woods. Judging from the amount of blood here, he's hurt pretty badly. We'll have him in custody soon. We can track him down from that. Glenhaven is no longer a safe place for him, thanks to you. He's bound to be heading for France."

"No, said Hill, a smile dawning across his face. "That's not where he's going. Tell him, Eve."

"Let me show you," she said and took them down to the huge map she was finishing on behalf of her father.

She quickly showed Whit the location identified by the coordinates—first using the Greenwich meridian as her point of origin. As Hill had predicted, the coordinates identified a location in the middle of the Bristol Channel off England's west coast. She then used the same coordinates, but started them from the Paris meridian which bisected France's capital city. This time the coordinates identified a location outside a tiny town southeast of London.

"That's where he is," said Eve. "I think you'll find that the sketch identifies a cottage in the area."

"Brilliant," said Whit. "Absolutely brilliant. Camberton, send word to Henson to bring all available men and meet us at my townhouse in London. Not only do we know where to look, but thanks to you we know exactly who we're looking for. All in all, things seem to be turning our way at last. Now I'm going to have a word with Lady Tangier. I have a few more questions that need answers."

Whit started down the stairs, but then turned as if suddenly remembering. "By the way, congratulate me, Camberton. I have a son!"

Epilogue

The gathering of the ladies—duchesses all—around the tea table in the first parlor of the Ice Duke's townhouse was not the normal social occasion.

The first thing they had dispensed with was the proliferation of "your gracing," as Linney called it. The Duchess of Easton had been the first to propose they move immediately to Christian names, considering they all had more than one connection to each other and also that their husbands were friends. More to the point, their husbands were at this very moment engaged in a manhunt that—with any luck at all—would lead at last to the capture of the infamous Monsieur Jones, now also known as Viscount Glenly.

Glenly was badly injured, thanks to the efforts of his former lover. Lady Tangier—soon to be the dowager Countess Tangier—was, even now, packing up her small household and moving to the continent. Her daughter was thrilled at this turn of events and couldn't have come up with a better solution if she'd thought about it for months.

"My mother can, as you might have heard, be a bit…let's say a bit overbearing." Eve told the other ladies.

Linney laughed at the understatement of the year. "Quite right. If she'd had her way about things, Eve would be married to my Avery. Evidently she had been planning that particular match for years."

"Since I was born," confirmed Eve with a laugh. "She is certainly a force to be reckoned with. I hope the continent is ready for her."

"If she misbehaves, we should send her to Saint Helena with Napoleon," said Henrianna as she rocked her daughter Rose to sleep. Rose had flatly refused to go anywhere away from her mother and, after several attempts, Henrianna had given in. Rose had made it clear that her mother was to have nothing to do with the other baby that everyone was making such a fuss over. Henrianna chuckled. "I'm afraid her nose is going to be very out of joint in about seven months," she confided to the ladies.

"Congratulations!" said Vivian. "That's wonderful news. I know Edgewood is pleased. If ever a man needed a big family, it is he. And I suppose there's always the chance that you will have twins?"

"Evidently the twins tend to appear with the men, not the ladies," said Henrianna. "Although Hill and I obviously are not identical twins, so I suppose there's always the possibility. Eve is the one who has the better chance."

"Not for a while, though, I hope," said Eve. "After we leave Linney and Avery in Greece, we're planning an extensive wedding trip to Italy. I can't wait to see some of the maps they have in Rome."

"Are you certain you don't want to come with us to see the pyramids?" Linney's itinerary grew longer with each passing day.

"We need to give you some time alone, don't you think?" said Eve. She looked up as the clock in the hallway struck the hour.

“Thompson,” said Vivian said to the butler who answered her summons. Please bring some more hot water for the ladies. I wonder why we haven’t heard anything yet.”

Thompson bowed. “Pardon me, your grace, but their graces have just returned. They should be here imminently.”

The ladies stood in anticipation and were rewarded by four rather rumpled, slightly muddied dukes entering the room.

“Tell us everything,” said Vivian. “Is he captured at last?”

“Even better,” said Edgewood, crossing the room to take his sleeping daughter from his wife. “He’s dead.”

“Are you certain?” Henrianna brushed back a lock of her husband’s hair as she asked her question.

“We made certain of it,” said Hill, stooping to kiss his wife. “I’m sorry, Eve. He was still your father.”

“He was never my father,” said Eve. “Not in any way that mattered. I do not mourn him and I will sleep better knowing that he is gone.”

“He was cunning until the end,” said Whit with one arm around his wife. He had already smoothed a wrinkled coverlet in his son’s cradle. “He was planning to travel to Saint Helena as a priest. I don’t know if the plan was to help Napoleon escape or to beatify him, but he had already set the plan in motion. Lucky for us he continued to have a low opinion of the Ice Duke and his merry men. But when he saw he was surrounded in his secret location, he decided death would be preferable to capture. I can’t say that I’m sorry. Finally the devil did something helpful. It would have been a difficult trial for the country.”

"And a difficult trial for the Ice Duke," said Avery with his arm around Linney's waist. "Or would you have enjoyed it?"

Whit did not answer, but merely raised one eyebrow and stared at his brother with an icy gaze.

Linney laughed. "You know your stare has no effect on your brother, Whit. Why do you even bother?"

Thompson appeared in the doorway with a tray holding eight empty goblets. A footman trailed behind him carrying several bottles of Whit's best champagne.

"A toast," said the Duke of Whitley, when everyone had a glass. "To all those who have given so much—too often their very lives—to bring down Napoleon's spymaster. To England and a lasting peace. God save the King!"

A word about the author...

Carolina Prescott is a writer of historical romances and the author of Haversham House Romances. She's always been a fan of a good romance, and her penchant for history—along with her love for a happy ending—makes writing historical romances a wonderfully logical career choice. “Everyone deserves a happy ending,” says Prescott, “and romance novels guarantee that every reader gets one.”

Carolina Prescott divides her time among places she loves, including Northern California, Michigan’s Upper Peninsula, and the Blue Ridge Mountains, but she always comes home to the house on a hill in her native North Carolina, where she is making a home for friends, family, and a very understanding Brittany spaniel.

You can visit her at carolinaprescott.com.

Thank you for purchasing
this publication of The Wild Rose Press, Inc.

For questions or more information
contact us at
info@thewildrosepress.com.

The Wild Rose Press, Inc.
www.thewildrosepress.com

www.ingramcontent.com/pod-product-compliance
Lightning Source LLC
Chambersburg PA
CBHW070110030726
47506CB00002B/678
* 9 7 8 1 5 0 9 2 6 0 7 2 0 *